Faded Glory:

A Tale of Yooperland

MARGARET L. SULLIVAN

CONTENTS

Chapter 1   Page 7

Chapter 2   Page 25

Chapter 3   Page 36

Chapter 4   Page 53

Chapter 5   Page 75

Chapter 6   Page 92

Chapter 7   Page 111

Epilogue   Page 128

CHAPTER 1

S he watched the sailboat round the point, struggling against the deep, gray swells that reflected the low, autumnal skies. "Unlikely," she thought. "Too late in the season. What fool is out there in a sailboat with a fall storm brewing?" Most sailing vessels were safely in their boat barns or at least hoisted out of the water before their owners fled south. Once she thought she too would flee south but life held her prisoner. "Maybe I'm like that sailboat," she mused, "wanting to flee but caught in the rolling whitecaps of the Lake. Maybe it's too late in my season."

As she watched the sailboat's slow progress against the winds and waves, her attention turned toward the long row of eight over eight windows that at once opened the house to nature and delineated the rustic space. "Dirty," she thought. "I'll have to have the windows cleaned before they come." The hours-old announcement of a visit filled her with surprise and foreboding.

"What the shit do they want?" was the first thing that crossed her mind.

She heard the kitchen door. "Bobby," she called knowing her son had returned from school.

"Mom," came the reassuring reply. "I'm hungry."

She walked into the kitchen. Living in a small town, or more precisely outside of a small town, she never had to explain. Everyone knew. The boy, the bastard son of Rob MacLeod, lived with his mother in the MacLeod summer cottage on a rocky cliff overlooking Lake Superior. Cottage was not a literal term in this case. The MacLeod place was approximately 10,000 square feet of log-encased space, including eight bedrooms and six baths. She had long ago closed off the majority of the mansion. In fact, she'd repeatedly told the MacLeods it would be more economically efficient for her and the boy to move into a modest house in town and simply close the house or sell the estate.

The MacLeod summer house sat on the watery edge of a sparsely populated land of deep forests and tiny hamlets known as Michigan's Upper Peninsula. The U.P., as it is commonly called, had only one "major metropolis," Marquette with a population of a bit over 21,000. In fact, Marquette County, 1,808 square miles of land with an additional 1,616 square miles underwater, reached its peak of population, little over 70,000, in 1980 and had been going downhill ever since.

Summer homes dotting the Lakeshore and smaller inland lakes swelled the population and employment during the short summer season when not only nature but also humanity seemed to come alive. The largest homes, like the MacLeod's, were the oldest, dating to an age when Detroit's automobile royalty sought to imitate the rustic Adirondacks cottages of New York's oligarchy. A lot of these families, she suspected the MacLeods included, now struggled to keep their aging odes to extravagance "in the family."

Maybe that was why the MacLeods had insisted she and the boy live in the summer home none of them had visited for six years. She'd wondered if they just didn't want to look at one of Rob's most glaring "screw-ups." That went double for Rob, who after a year of telling the world he had sired a son, simply disappeared into an alcoholic fueled oblivion. She would gladly nominate Rob for the world's worst father if such an honor existed.

"I have some news for you," she said. Bobby looked up from his peanut butter and jelly sandwich. "Your grandparents are coming to visit for a few days."

"Why? We see them every Sunday for dinner. Is something wrong with their house?"

"No, not my parents. Your father's parents. They want to see you."

"Why? I don't even know them."

"I know. Sometimes, as people get older, they have more time to do the things they always wanted to do."

"They live in Detroit, don't they?"

"Outside Detroit. I think they spend a lot of time in Florida lately."

"Do they have other grandchildren? Do they see them like we see Grandma and Grandpa Flannigan?"

"I don't think they have other grandchildren, not that I know of anyway. Your father is their only child."

"Is he coming too?"

"No, not that I know of."

"They're just coming to see me?"

"That's what your grandfather said." Of course, she wasn't going to tell her nine-year-old son that she didn't believe his paternal grandfather. For the past couple of hours she'd mused over other possibilities. The first on her list was the family fortunes had waned to a point they were going to sell the place and cut off her allowance/salary for managing the estate. If they cut her off completely, she didn't know how she was going to support the boy on the U.P.'s weak economy and certainly didn't want to take him away from the only family he knew.

Now that Bobby had asked about Rob, other possibilities came to mind. Maybe they were going to tell her Rob was dead, or married, or had sired other illegitimate children. She wondered if she would feel anything in any of those cases.

"I guess I'll have to call your Aunt Jennie and Uncle Jim to come over and help me get the place ready for guests. I wonder how many rooms they'll need and how much food they'll want. Maybe we can put Jennie on the payroll as part-time cook." She was talking to herself as much as to her son. "Guess we'll have to drive into Marquette for supplies." She envisioned a leisurely hour drive now that the usual summer people and random tourists had gone. On the way she'd pass Granot Loma, the largest house in Michigan with its 26,000 square feet and 50 rooms. Priced at $40 million, the place had been on the market for years. Maybe Bobby would be in college before the MacLeods could sell their place.

◆ ◆ ◆

"We're in good shape," she declared as Jennie and Jim walked toward the kitchen door. "I'll put both of you down for maintenance….say $15 per hour?" It was more of a statement than a question. Jennie cooked at one of the local inns during the summer and on some winter weekends while Jim did maintenance for the local school district. With three boys, they had a hard time making financial ends meet. In fact, most Yoopers, as natives of the Upper Peninsula were called, would have thought poverty was the natural state of things if it was not for the summer people. "I'll put you on the books for cooking while they are here, but I don't quite know their plans. Could be a couple of hours or a full week."

"As soon as you figure out what they want, give me a call. The suspense is killing me."

"They're going to sell," Jim said. "These places are a maintenance nightmare. You haven't let them know how this place is deteriorating. Tens of thousands of dollars of work should be done."

"I know. I guess I figured if the place gets too expensive, they'd be annoyed and blame me. God only knows they blamed me for getting pregnant."

"I remember," Jennie laughed. "I also remember you telling his parents what they could do with themselves when they suggested you were trying to snare their innocent little boy."

"Innocent," she laughed. "I told them I liked Rob in spite of the fact that he had shitty, alcoholic parents but wasn't stupid enough to think Rob would ever be husband material. Apparently the rich girl who made the mistake of marrying him figured that out pretty quick."

"At least they did right by you."

"Right? Since their company owned this place, my salary was a business expense, not something that came out of their pockets. They gave their grandson the bare minimum; a place to live and just enough money to keep him in food and clothing. But not even a birthday card. Sure hope they, or Rob, come up with college tuition."

"Could be worse," Jennie said. "When the company went bankrupt, at least they kept this place.'

"That's because the banks didn't want to be stuck with it. Maybe they've found a buyer after all."

"We'll find out on Wednesday. You'll be at Mom's tomorrow?"

"Of course. She'd be mad if we don't come. She's still mad at Don and Carol for moving to Houston and Detroit.

"We'll be going. Bobby coming home soon?"

"In an hour or so. Emma Williams said she'd drop him off after the birthday party."

She watched her sister and brother-in-law drive toward the road before going into the massive great room where the windows now sparkled. She scanned the Lake. The light was already fading although it was only a little after five in the afternoon. Her mother had objected to her moving to the MacLeod's 125 acres of forest with only an infant for company. She had a rifle and a handgun and knew how to use them. And the Sheriff's number was programmed into her phone.

Sometimes it was incredibly lonely but she'd survived on frequent visits by her numerous relatives. On Thanksgiving and Christmas she stayed in a basement bedroom that had once been her brother's, before he finished college and moved to Texas. Now when he visited, his family stayed at a local Inn.

When she heard a car coming down the driveway, she thought Bobby was early. Going to the kitchen door she watched the unfamiliar sports car come to a halt. Rob stepped out, and smiled. Only the crunch of recently fallen leaves beneath his feet shattered the silence as he walked toward her.

"What the fuck are you doing here?"

He didn't answer until she stood aside to let him into the kitchen. "Nice to see you too, Meagan." He looked around. "Place hasn't changed at all. I'm here for the big family pow-wow. Thought I'd come early so we can get our stories straight. Not sure the Old Man knows I'm coming."

She followed him into the great room where he threw a small suitcase on a sofa and began switching on lamps dating from his youth. He didn't look much different. Not tall and rather square, he was still trim although his once straight shoulders seemed to slump a bit. His face still housed a strong, square chin and clear blue eyes. Only the blond hair seemed to recede a bit. Still a good-looking man, she thought.

"I presume you want a drink." His jacket followed the suitcase. He was wearing one of his trademark light blue sweaters that emphasized the color of his eyes.

"Coffee if you have it. Just got out of rehab. I made life so miserable for my loving wife she reluctantly committed me and then happily divorced me. Or is in the process; I don't know. I went a little crazy and caused an embarrassing scene. One of my finest, if I don't say so myself."

She started to the kitchen. "I thought she divorced you years ago."

"Different wife, different divorce."

"Hard to keep track," she called as she put coffee in the filter. "Since we never hear from you."

"Guess you're mad at me too." He settled into a chair by the fireplace.

She stood in the doorway between the kitchen and great room. "Yes, I'm mad at you. Why are you such a shitty father?"

"Because I'm a shitty person. I mess everything up. My father now refers to me as 'Mr. Screw Up.' Of course I'm a shitty father. My father was a shitty father. Don't know about my grandfather but my guess is he was pretty shitty, too."

"That's no excuse." The words were sheer Rob. He'd figured out long ago that if he denigrated himself, the other person had nowhere to go but agree with him. Besides, she couldn't throw him out of his family's house. She threw her hands in the air and went back to the kitchen.

When she handed him the coffee, she noticed a slight twitch. "Having a hard time?" she tried to be sympathetic.

"Yeah. I've been in and out of rehab so many times it's almost a joke. I'm a little twitchy. Sex might help. Want to have sex with me?"

"NO. ABSOLUTELY NOT. "

"I was afraid you'd say that."

"It's Saturday. Go into Thunder Bay and pick up someone in a bar. I'd prefer you didn't bring her back here but if you do, be quiet. Your son lives here too."

"Can't go to a bar. Have to stay sober while the parents are here. Guess I'll have a week of sobriety and abstinence."

"Won't kill you."

"It might."

"What do they want?"

"My parents? My father came up with a doozy this time. He not only wants you to take care of this house but his messed up son as well. He long ago decided I'm worthless, an embarrassment at his country clubs, both in Detroit and in Florida. I have not been able to stay married or produce a legitimate heir, much less handle any job he's given me. He's also decided you are a stable woman who could be a good influence...."

"Don't tell me he wants you to live here so I can be your glorified babysitter."

"Worse than that, he thinks you should be my glorified wife. Having a wife, even a Yooper, and a newly legitimate son would make me a little more presentable to his friends, especially those who don't already know me." While the natives of the U.P. used the term, "Yooper" sounded denigrating on outside tongues. "And when alcoholism, or whatever, rears its ugly head, we can retreat up here where you have connections."

"You have to be kidding."

"Nope. Not only that but he doesn't trust me with what is left of the rapidly diminishing family fortune. He wants to put it in trust for his only grandson with you as one of the trustees."

"What changed his mind about the slutty Yooper who got pregnant to entrap his little boy?"

"Age. Desperation. A detective's report saying you are a stable, dependable person who is good with a buck and doesn't have any obvious vices. And a grandson who doesn't show any signs of the genetic family weaknesses and is even a good student. A real family first. It's his last gasp, his attempt to keep the family alive and respectable."

"So that's who that guy was. He asked so many questions about me my brother-in-law and a couple of my cousins nearly threw him out of town."

"Do you want to marry me, Meagan?"

"No. I've always liked you. My mistake was having sex with you. I know you well enough to know you are not a good prospective husband. And I'm sure you don't want to marry me."

"You'd be crazy to marry me. I'm a liar and a cheat. I've always been a coward. And yet, unlike my other wives, you'd know what you would be getting. Think of it as a business deal. "

As teenagers, she had tried to cheer him up by telling him he was worthwhile; that he was just suffering youthful doubts. Of course, at the time she didn't understand the depths of his alcoholism. Now cheerfulness seemed an exercise in futility.

"Mom," the back door slammed. "Whose car is outside?"

Rob was on his feet as Bobby entered the great room. He held out his hand. "Hello, you must be Robert James MacLeod IV. I'm Robert James MacLeod III."

Bewildered, Bobby looked up but ignored Rob's hand. "You're my daddy?"

"Seems so, young man. Maybe your mother will get you a pop or something while you sit down and tell me what you like to do. We have to plan some fun things while I am here."

"How long are you going to be here?"

"That depends on your mother."

"Oh no, don't tell him that. You can stay as long as you like, Rob. It's your house." She resisted the urge to scream, *Don't do this to him. Don't be charming; don't give him hope of having a normal father because we both know you won't stay. Please, don't do this to him.*

Worse yet, what was she going to do with Rob tomorrow? Going to her parents' house without him left a lonely man in a big house with a full bar. Her family considered him a pariah, which would make for an uncomfortable evening where all the adults would be drinking. The thought of what to do with him in a land where everyone drank too much ended any thought of marrying him for the money. No amount of cash would ever be worth it.

"Maybe tomorrow," she said, "we could drive to Marquette for a movie and dinner."

"But we always go to Grandma's for dinner on Sundays."

"Yes, but since your Dad is here," she forced a smile, "we ought to do something really special. Just the three of us."

Bobby nodded but didn't look particularly happy about it.

♦♦♦

Sunday went better than Meagan had hoped. Of course, both her sister and mother objected to her being alone in the big house with Rob MacLeod. He had the reputation of being a violent drunk, which he was under the right circumstances. Sometimes those circumstances were external and obvious, but at other times they seemed internal and inexplicable. But he'd never been violent with her. Most of the time. She pushed away a memory of him shoving her aside so hard she bruised the side of her face and scraped her shoulder on a pine tree as she slumped to the ground. She'd been trying to keep him from Matt Johansen whom he'd beaten badly before three other boys pulled him away.

In true Rob style the next morning, he had arrived at her house full of remorse and apologies. "Shit, Meagan, you're the last person I want to hurt. You're my best friend in the U.P. I can always count on you. If there is anything I can do, if money or anything would help... You shouldn't have gotten in the way. That fucking Matt said something about my mother and I just couldn't stop myself."

In her teenage naïveté, she excused his bad behavior on outside forces that occasionally overwhelmed him. After all, he was her friend, her mentor, the coolest of cool kids who introduced her to the world where outside money and poor Yoopers met. He was her entrée into summers of boathouse parties, beach bashes, and country bars where underage drinkers congregated. She swore to her friends, as she had sworn to her parents, that she had stumbled on a rock when she tried to separate Rob from Matt. Reportedly Robert James MacLeod, Jr. paid Matt Johansen's parents $10,000 to fix Matt's teeth and forget the whole incident.

At 30 years of age, Meagan wasn't so easily fooled. She knew as long as Rob was sober, he would be mostly charming. But there were signs; fidgeting, pacing, unsettled thoughts or fragmented conversations indicating when he was finding sobriety unbearable. If the signs appeared, she promised herself, she would take Bobby and flee to her parents' house where she would be surrounded by an army of relatives.

There were none of those signs on their Sunday in Marquette. Rob was in a good mood, smiling repeatedly at the boy, and asking him questions. They took Bobby to see "Diary of a Wimpy Kid," which he loved. They wandered the mall where Rob bought Bobby some books and an elaborate Lego Set. He insisted upon buying his son a coat and tie for his meeting with his grandparents. Then they went to Elizabeth's Chop House where Rob spent a week of her usual grocery money on oysters and a rib-eye steak. She had the cheaper whitefish while Rob insisted the chef depart from the menu to serve the boy a hamburger and fries. He only glanced longingly at the wine list but ordered club soda with lemon instead.

The moon was bright on the way home. Bobby fell asleep in the cramped back seat of the sports car. "Nice," he said. "I'd forgotten how nice this place is and how easy you are to be with. I haven't seen you in what...six or seven years...and yet we can talk like I've seen you every day. Maybe the old man is on to something."

"It's only late September. Wait until the snow flies and everything ices over. Then life isn't so good. Then I won't be so easy to talk to. The sky, the Lake, everything turns gray until enough of the Lake freezes to turn off the 'Lake Superior Snow Machine.' Then the sun can come out and make the icy world pretty again, if you can call a hundred plus inches of snow pretty." What she meant was the long brutal, winters were no place for people with mood swings or emotional problems.

"You Yoopers used to talk about how you loved the winters....cross-country skiing, ice skating, snowmobiles and even dog sleds. What really sounded like fun was drag racing on the frozen lake. You talked about skiing on Marquette Mountain like it was the fucking Alps."

"That's because none of us ever expected to see the Rockies much less the Alps. We had to use our imaginations."

"You talked like you wouldn't leave for anything."

"We lied. We'd have happily left. We envied your fancy schools and talk of what you'd do in Florida at Christmas. We lied to you and maybe we even lied to ourselves. Winter up here is an ordeal you'd hate. By spring we'd want to kill each other."

"Are you trying to tell me something?"

"I'm not trying. I'm telling you that you wouldn't survive a winter here."

"Are you trying to get rid of me already?"

"I'm trying to tell you the things we didn't tell you snobby summer people when we were young. There's a reason our alcoholism rate is so high and now have increasing meth and heroin problems. There's a reason Yoopers commit suicide in March and April. There's a reason I can name families where fathers have been jailed for incest and why people start swapping mates before winter is over. It's boredom; the bone numbing cold and mind chilling thought that winter is never going to end."

She didn't add that part of the reason for agreeing to live in the isolation of the MacLeod place was to shield her son from the worst of Yooper life. When relatives got too drunk or started talking about the more unsavory parts of life, she could take Bobby away from it all. If he understood he might be heir to a better life, he might escape late winter despair.

"I always thought of these were happy little towns."

"If we told you the truth, you'd have closed your fancy houses and taken your jobs south with you. There's so much illegal hunting here because people are hungry. Most people don't fish from ice shacks because they like the cold. By spring we're broke. Summer people are an important part of what is left of the local economy."

"What else didn't you Yoopers tell us civilized people?" She'd long known people from the Lower Peninsula, or Trolls as Yoopers called them because they lived below the Mackinac Bridge, and considered denizens of the U.P. semi-barbaric. "I thought the locals and the summer people, especially the kids, got along well."

"We locals were exhausted. You rich kids partied all night, slept all morning, swam all afternoon, and showed up on the beaches and in the boathouses every sundown ready to party. We got up early because we had at least one, and often several, summer jobs. We worked all day through hangovers or sleeplessness and then tried to keep up with you at night. But you never seemed to notice."

"So you envied us? Hated us? Loved us?"

"A little of all of the above Plus we resented the shit out of you for showing us another world we'd never have. In some cases it made us study hard as a way out of here but most of us...myself included...stumbled along that path. The best way was through marriage but, as we often said among ourselves, 'we try to marry those rich bastards but they aren't as stupid as they seem'."

"But you didn't try to force me to marry you when you were holding an infant in one hand and a DNA test saying I was the father in the other."

"No I didn't, but most of the girls around here would have and your parents would have been right as to motive."

"What made you different?"

I've always been a realist. You're the romantic."

"That's questionable."

"Why?" she asked.

"Remember how we used to sit out at that old tavern on Clearwater Lake and talk about being in love? I was always in love..."

"For about two weeks at a time. The only thing that changed was the name of the girl."

"You weren't any better.... in love at least twice a summer. God only knows what you did during the winter." He realized they'd both lived split lives. His was divided into Detroit, the U.P., and Florida. His first morning in each place felt like a continuation of a parallel life. Hers was split into short summers and long winters. The local kids, or townies, never talked about their winters in any meaningful way. Now he wondered what really happened when the summer people left.

"You realize," her voice caught his attention, "that both of us were really just in love with falling in love."

"So several shrinks have told me. They always want you to bare your soul at those rehab places. According to my parents' hired spy, you haven't been involved with anyone since the boy was born."

"When they put him in my arms, I suddenly realized I was responsible for another human being and didn't want to screw him up. I'd seen a lot of single mothers with a parade of men in and out of their houses and what it did to their kids. I swore I'd never be that woman; that my goal would be to give Bobby the best life I could."

"Shit, you're noble. I never noticed noble about you before. You used to be fun. I might be able to survive the winter but I don't think I could survive righteous nobility. That would drive any man to drink."

"Thanks for the vote of confidence, Rob. You really haven't changed."

A voice interrupted them from the barely existing back seat. "Mom, are we home yet?"

Rob carried a sleepy Bobby to his bed. "Why are you and the kid sleeping in the servants' bedrooms?"

"Because I'm a servant."

"Your son has the MacLeod name."

"It's a matter of practicality. We nearly froze the first winter. These little rooms are warmer and face southeast. That way the winter wind coming across the Lake doesn't come through the cracks on this side of the buildings. I've spent the last two summers forcing chink between the logs and I'm not finished yet."

"Why don't you just have it done?"

"Your parents haven't gotten over the shock of putting a fifty thousand dollar roof on the house. I don't know why they don't sell the place."

"It reminds them of their glory days. They hate to give it up, even if they never come here anymore. Maybe there's another solution. I noticed Granot Loma rents rooms and party spaces."

She shrugged. "Your parents might consider that too crass and commercial."

"Dear old Dad might like the idea better if it came from you and not Mr. Screw-Up. That is if he likes you as much as he wants to. To think that little Meagan Flannigan from some God-forsaken spot outside Thunder Bay in the U.P. is the last hope of the mighty MacLeods. Life is sure fucked up."

♦ ♦ ♦

Two days later Rob was still surprisingly sober as he left to pick up his parents at Sawyer International Airport in Marquette, somewhat of a misnomer as the small airport, a remnant of a Cold War air force base, only connected the U.P.'s "major metropolis" with Detroit, Chicago, and Minneapolis via planes of 50 or less seats. Once the MacLeods would have arrived by private plane but now had been reduced to commercial flight. According to Rob, they'd traded their estate on Lake St. Claire in Grosse Pointe Shores for a condo in Harrison Township at the north end of the same Lake for their increasingly infrequent forays to Detroit. Instead they spent most of their time at their palatial beach house in Palm Beach.

Meagan glanced at the long, two story Great Room thinking it had the look of antiquity revisited, like an old lady donning her hat and gloves to go shopping at Walmart. Long dead animals stared down on them as she and Jennie awaited the arrival of the elder MacLeods. The pine furniture had long since seen its best days, and the sofas and easy chairs slouched toward the end of their usefulness. Wondering if the flue was still working properly, Meagan watched the fire flicker in the massive fireplace constructed of stones dragged by ancient glaciers from God-only-knows-where before being washed smooth by the Lake. The flames gave life to the room. If Rob really wanted to turn this place into a bed and breakfast, he could advertise it as "Vintage North Woods: Your Trip to the Past."

A balcony across the room from the massive fireplace linked three large bedrooms and two baths while the hallway below led to the master suite and three smaller rooms, each with their own baths. She'd closed the heating vents and water supply to all of the family bedrooms and baths so long ago that her brother-in-law had trouble opening them.

The servants' quarter behind the massive fireplace was enough for her and Bobby. The small kitchen, built for utility, left Meagan's friends and family laughing at the pre- World War II space. Their life revolved around the adjacent sitting room, complete with wood burning stove for added winter warmth. She liked to think of the room as cozy but it was crowded by a table and chairs where Bobby was now doing his homework, a television on a small buffet and a sofa she'd bought for comfort. Two small bedrooms separated by a barebones bathroom completed the area. In the summers, she and Bobby sometimes sat in the great room or wandered out to the screened porch off the dining room but on winter nights Meagan loved sitting close to Bobby as they watched the television or played the board games. Jennie repeatedly warned her she hovered too much, thus setting herself up for eventual abandonment when Bobby reached an age where he'd rather be with his friends than his mother. She didn't want to think of a life alone.

"Can't wait for this ordeal to be over," Jennie broke the silence. "Can't imagine they want you to live here while Rob is in the house." Meagan hadn't told Jennie about the notion of marriage because she knew her family would worry that she might actually do it. "Are you sure you're all right with him here?"

"I'm all right. He hasn't tried to get into my bed if that is what you are thinking. He's been very sober and gets along well with Bobby. I just wonder about his parents. If I remember correctly, they were drunk most of the time, although Rob said his father has been on the wagon for the past two years. I really don't have any good memories of them. His mother called me every name in the book...and then made up some more."

When they heard Meagan's old car, Jennie went to the kitchen and Bobby stood close to his mother. The elder Mr. MacLeod's newfound sobriety showed. He was erect, and dour, reminding Meagan of a scowling school master from some English movie. His wife's drunkenness was just as apparent. She was short, so the thirty or forty pounds she had gained in the years since Megan had last seen her, swelled the middle of her body into a flabby ball. Her overdone makeup was smeared and her graying hair pushed into a sloppy bun on the top of her head, a long mink coat haphazardly falling from her shoulder. "God awful airplane," she was complaining as she walked into the door. "Squeezed in like sardines. Hardly human. Don't know how people do it. I need a martini."

Rob headed toward the bar but Meagan quickly cut him off. "I'll do it. Introduce Bobby." As she reached for the gin, the elder MacLeod cleared his throat. "Nice strong handshake for a young man. Bodes well for your character."

"Thank you, sir. I'm pleased to see you again, although I don't remember seeing you before."

"Yes. It has been too long. But we'll see if we can rectify that. Perhaps you would like to spend Christmas in Florida with your grandmother and me."

"Thank you sir, but I couldn't possibly leave my mother alone during the holidays. I do appreciate your offer."

Meagan smiled as she turned with the martini. Thanks to Rob's coaching, Bobby sounded like something out of the last century. Maybe the coat and tie were good ideas. Mary MacLeod took the drink without acknowledging Meagan's existence.

"You've done a nice job with the boy," Robert MacLeod addressed Meagan. "I hope the boy is having dinner with us."

"Of course, he is." Rob had spent the night before instructing Bobby on proper table manners. "Dinner will be rather simple; I wasn't sure what you'd expect. Can I get you a club soda or something? Rob has been drinking club soda."

"Good. Good, that's fine. Simple dinner. Rustic place. A little shabbier than I remembered. Maybe we can spend some time here next summer, spruce the place up."

Rob looked at Meagan but she knew it was too soon to bring up any commercial ideas. Instead Robert looked at his wife who had settled into a sofa near the dark windows. "If possible, I'd like to eat soon. Mary seems a little tired and needs to go to bed."

"Don't be telling me what to do. God Almighty, but you're dull since you quit drinking. Rob, have a little drink with me." Rob didn't reply but Meagan went to the kitchen to tell Jennie to hurry dinner.

As they sat in the two story dining room adjacent to the great room, Mary MacLeod complained about the furniture, the lack of light outside, the chinaware, the old wood and smoky smell of the house, and the lack of her favorite wines. In fact, the wine was so bad that she was forced to continue drinking martinis. About the fifth time she used the term "God-awful," Bobby looked at her and asked, "Why does God think so many things are awful?" which brought the night's only smile to his grandfather's face.

After dinner they sat in the great room until she told Bobby it was time for him to go to bed. Robert looked at Rob. "Escort your mother to her room and don't come back." The brusqueness of his order startled Meagan and brought a flash of anger to Rob's face. He rose and took his almost limp mother by the arm.

"Miss Flannigan," Robert MacLeod stared at her. "I may have been wrong about you. My wife is a drunk and my son is worthless. Can't seem to do anything right. Sometimes I wonder if he's really mine."

"You underestimate Rob, Mr. MacLeod. He has problems but he also has potential."

"Are you fond of him?"

"I've been fond of him since I was fifteen."

"I didn't know he was coming here until yesterday. I wanted to see you and the boy alone before I made any decisions. You've done a fine job with that young man. He's polite and mentally sharp. Can't ask for much more these days. I'd like to get to know him better. Perhaps it would be better if you both come to Florida for a while this winter."

"I'll have to think about that. I don't want to take Bobby out of school for any extended time. I have a very large family here, so Bobby is used to a lot of family at Christmas. I appreciate your taking an interest in my son and your generosity," the last word almost stuck in her throat, "that has allowed me to live here without having to work outside the house. I appreciate the fact that

I am always here when he goes to school and when he comes home. But to be perfectly honest, my fear at this point is the MacLeods will take an interest in him for a while and then forget about him. That could do a lot of damage to him."

"I don't think that will happen. He's all I have left."

Meagan looked into Robert MacLeod's eyes. "He's all I've ever had."

"He's my only hope to carry on the family name. I wasn't too happy when Rob insisted upon putting MacLeod on the birth certificate but now I'm glad he did."

"Thank you for that. But you have Rob too."

"Have I? I'd say his mother spoiled him but mostly we both ignored him until he got into trouble. Then we got him out of trouble and went back to ignoring him. He's thirty-three years old and has never been able to hold a job, not ones I gave him before the bankruptcy or the ones my friends gave him. He's been married three times, always a disaster. It's as if he goes out of his way to humiliate the girls he marries…and two of them came from nice families. I know alcoholism runs in the family and I'm no saint. In fact, I've done terrible things but Rob loses all self-control when he drinks. I have scars to prove it. And I fear drugs are involved too. He's almost run through a trust fund that would have lasted a prudent man for a lifetime. Several years ago my lawyer talked him into signing a binding agreement giving him a small income for the rest of his life rather than the principle. He won't starve or be homeless. Consequently I don't want to leave the MacLeod money in his hands. I've had my lawyer and my accountant look through every bill you've ever sent me and how you've spent the small salary I give you. They concluded you are scrupulously honest and financially prudent. I sent that roofing bill to three contractors, one in Detroit and two in Florida. They all said I got a good deal, better than they could give me. So I'd like to pursue getting to know you and my grandson. If all goes well, I'd like to leave the money and properties in trust to Bobby."

"That's very kind of you. But please don't mention money to Bobby. I never want him to feel that he's on probation, or even a potential heir to anything. That would not make for a good relationship. All I'd ask at this point is you guarantee Bobby's tuition at whatever university he chooses. Then I think he can have the satisfaction of making his way in the world."

Robert MacLeod didn't catch the irony of her wanting Bobby to "have the satisfaction of making his way in the world," something neither Rob nor his father had to do. Neither was the better for their hereditary privilege. Rob saw his family wealth as both a protection and a curse. The Old Man belonged to a generation of men who were born wealthy but somehow though that they had earned their success. Delusion wasn't the sole province of the mentally impaired poor.

"You want a successful son," the elder MacLeod answered, "and I want a successful MacLeod. The two are not mutually exclusive."

"There is another thing, Mr. MacLeod. I'd like you to give Rob another chance. This place needs a lot of work but it could be a successful bed & breakfast or an inn. It was Rob's idea and I think a good idea. Rob might not be good at sitting in an office and looking at numbers but he's a natural born host." She consciously didn't qualify the statement with "as long as he's relatively sober." Instead she went on, "It won't make a fortune but it might pay for itself. Even if it doesn't, I'm sure your attorney could find a way to make it a tax deduction. I think you ought to let Rob give it a try."

"And you'll stay here with him and oversee whatever he does? "

"Yes," she knew she was taking a chance, not only with her life but with her son's as well.

"It's an idea. These places are dinosaurs. Nobody wants them anymore. If I could have gotten a decent price I would have sold a long time ago. Didn't get half of what I thought the Grosse Pointe property was worth and don't want to let this place go that way too."

"Perhaps we could get some preliminary figures on costs and market potential."

"If you can keep Rob interested in the project, it might be worth it. To be honest, since you and Rob have known each other for so long, I was hoping you'd rekindle the spark that must have once existed between you."

"I hate to disappoint you, Mr. MacLeod, but Rob and I were simply friends. Then one particularly bad day in my life Rob showed up at my student apartment in Marquette. He was also having a bad time, so I invited him to stay. That spark, as you put it, lasted for about a week. I ended up pregnant but he was off again. I was surprised he answered my e-mail."

"Too bad. I would welcome you into the MacLeod Family. Maybe you can stir up a spark in him again. It would be worth your while."

"No, sir. That I will not do for money. That wouldn't be fair to any of us."

CHAPTER 2

T he forest enveloped Rob as he fled the house, his parents, and Meagan and headed down the path toward what they'd always called the swimming lake. Rob couldn't remember if it had a real name. While the birch and maples near the house had mostly shed their leaves, the inland forest became increasingly coniferous, thick, and foreboding. While the bright sunshine flooded the area along the Lake, it barely penetrated the stands of pine. Funny, he didn't remember it this way. In his youth, the mile long path had been wider and weed-free, with small pebbles singing beneath his feet.

Meagan might have kept the main house from falling in on itself, Rob thought, but she hadn't done shit with the grounds and outbuildings. Yesterday he'd visited the boathouse half expecting to see the vintage wooden Chris-Craft motorboat and Cheoy Lee sailboat that had been sold long ago. The roof of the two-bedroom apartment over the boathouse was near collapse. The party barn just east of the main house wasn't in much better shape. The floor definitely tilted toward the Lake while the old billiard table was ruined and the ping-pong table warped. He hadn't tried the single bowling lane or the old electronic games, but was sure that none of them worked.

The complex was designed for parties. Guests were encouraged to wander the estate, going from the main bar, which was always in the boathouse, to the buffet, which was always in the dining room of the main house. The great room had a smaller service bar, as did the party barn. Sometimes a bar popped up on the lawn in case guests needed a drink along the way. When his mother envisioned a tropical luau in the boreal forest, workmen lined the path to the swimming lake with torches where a temporary tiki hut served rum drinks garnished with tacky little paper umbrellas or tiny plastic swords skewering chunks of pineapple. With so many bars in stark contrast to a single food station, Rob wondered how they expected him to become anything other than an alcoholic.

A prehistoric glacier created the swimming lake by digging a five-acre basin and filling it with melt water. It didn't quite match his memories either. The wide sandy beach was narrower than he recalled and strewn with forest waste. The remnants of summer-time water lilies and pickerel grew within the old swimming area while aquatic weeds quivered beneath the water's surface.

When he was very young, a swimming raft floated a short distance from shore and colorful beach toys and fluffy towels littered the white sand. Later, bonfires cast long shadows of milling teenagers toward the darkness of the forest. Rob smiled at the memory of being surrounded by friends getting high on beer and pot, saying and doing stupid things, and wandering off into the woods or backseats of cars. Some couples didn't even bother with that, and just moved to the edges of the firelight. It had been a great place; first for swimming in relatively warmth and safety and then for youthful parties hidden from adult eyes. Rob gloried in the memory of being the center of it all. Now he felt as old and as neglected as this place.

Rob sat on a log and removed a carefully concealed joint from his pocket, rationalizing this as a way to calm his nerves. Without it, he'd start drinking or explode. He remembered his father suffering a heart attack shortly before one of his mother's elaborate parties. As the ambulance started down the driveway on the long trip to the hospital in Marquette, his mother loudly and bitterly complained, "the Bastard did this just to ruin my party." Rob remembered having two reactions. First, he was surprised when his mother actually cancelled the event. Second, he hoped his father would die.

He hated the Old Man. He'd hated him for as long as he could remember. While that was an indisputable, Rob never believed several psychiatrists' assertion that he was also always trying to please his father. His parents' screaming formed the soundtrack of his earliest memories, his father hurling verbal invectives and occasionally physically striking his mother. Rob would run to protect her. In one brutal instance, his father had thrown him across the room calling him a "little bastard" before Rob knew the meaning of the word. He told himself the Old Man hit him from time to time because he was protecting his mother, which was a kinder truth than that his father simply did not like him.

Whatever. He'd had his revenge several months ago. During one of the Old Man's increasingly frequent lectures on Rob's shortcomings, both as a son and a human being, years of pent up rage erupted. The police only released Rob from handcuffs after the family's Florida lawyer arrived. Then in true MacLeod fashion, a private doctor took the Old Man to a private hospital. A private security guard escorted Rob to rehab where he stayed for almost two months. His mother called several times but said that she was "too sick" to visit either her husband or her son. What she meant, Rob knew, was "too drunk."

He scanned the little lake again. Something moved in the woods across the water. Rob took a deep drag. He knew what was going on. It became crystal clear last night when his father insultingly dismissed him and his mother. Sobriety only made the Old Man's scheming worse. His father was using Meagan and the boy to punish him. He was threatening to replace Rob with Bobby. As he took his mother to the bedroom, she had warned him, "stay away from that girl....a gold digger if I ever saw one. The Old

Bastard is mean enough to disinherit you in favor of your little bastard. And that girl knows it. Wasn't the first time a MacLeod man was taken in by one of these harlots. Your father had a son up here too but his father had enough class not to let that Indian girl into the family. Even your father was smart enough to know that you don't marry someone like that."

Rob knew. When he was thirteen or fourteen some of the local boys taunted him. "Your brother lives around L'Anse. He can outrun anyone, bring down a deer with a bow and arrow, and is the quarterback on the high school football team. So, White Boy, what can you do, other than spend your daddy's money?" Rob learned of his half brother's death in Afghanistan from the Marquette Mining Journal.

And what the shit was he going to do about Meagan? He remembered the first time he had seen her behind the old fashioned marble counter in Ye Olde Ice Cream Shoppe in Thunder Bay, a hamlet about ten miles down the road with an additional three bars, two churches, a convenience/souvenir store, an old inn, and a gas station. "Cute" was his first thought. She still had the same big eyes that shifted from light brown to almost green and masses of chestnut brown hair. She had a Yooper complexion; pale, smooth, and white revealing her summers working indoors rather than lounging on beaches or in sailboats. She was shorter than he was, something he always liked in a female. A small waist, along with the tight tee shirt beneath the ruffled apron-uniform, emphasized the size of her breasts.

He ordered coffee and started a conversation. He was not pleased to discover she was Don Flannigan's little sister. Don was not only tall and tough, but did not hide his disdain for summer Trolls from beneath the Mackinac Bridge. Don later passed him in a crowded bar, ominously muttering, "mess with my little sister and I'll beat the shit out of you." In fact, when Meagan told him that she was pregnant, Rob envisioned Don Flannigan bashing down his front door.

Most local teenagers kept any negative opinions of the summer people to themselves. Friendships, real or pretend, meant invitations to parties where the beer and pot were free. Similarly, affluent teens understood they were expected to pay the bills in restaurants or bars. Rob wondered if the other summer residents shared his unspoken feeling the locals were really laughing at them. In their attempts to inject themselves into the local setting and allay their fears of not "measuring up," the summer-only teens never openly questioned whether the natives were lying to them. He recalled that Meagan lied at their first meeting. When Rob asked, Meagan added a year to her age and said "sixteen." When he asked if she had a boyfriend, she said "yes." Since he never saw signs of a serious boyfriend as Meagan flirted with one summer visitor after another, he wondered if she lied about that too.

In those days she was funny and always laughed at his jokes. He started going by the Ice Cream Shoppe on boring afternoons to talk to her. Sometimes, if not otherwise occupied, he swung by the Shoppe to give her a ride home. By their second summer, they'd drive to an old saloon on Clearwater Lake where no one asked questions about age. Over Rob's late afternoon beers and her orange pops, they analyzed their love lives, their futures, and the meaning of life. In retrospect, he did most of the talking.

Whenever neither of them was romantically involved, they'd go to parties together. If Rob wanted to leave with a girl who had promised sex, she'd just laugh. He was always a gentleman, meaning he drove Meagan home first or arranged for someone else to do so. If she wanted to leave with someone, Rob would tell the young man he had better get Meagan home safely.

It wasn't that he didn't think of Meagan in sexual terms. He did. Once when rather drunk, he clearly expressed his desires. She laughed and said, "I'm not crazy. I know how you treat your girlfriends and I don't want to be one of them. How many times have I heard you call a girl, tell her you couldn't make it because something has come up, and you'd explain later. You not only do not call again, you spend the rest of the summer avoiding her. I'll be your friend, thank you, because that lasts a lot longer." He knew she was right. Sex was easy but cute, adoring little sister substitutes were rare.

He inhaled the pot again. That was Meagan then. Meagan now had lost something of her smile and lot of the adoring. She was still an attractive woman although her waist had notably thickened. He wondered why there had been no men in her life. If the detective was right, he was probably the last man in her bed. Maybe he'd ruined her in some way. He strained to remember the week they'd shared but the memory was shrouded in cheap booze, pot smoke, and stale pizza. He didn't recall her as being bad in bed. Maybe she was frigid and he had been too stoned to notice.

He wasn't certain how much he liked her anymore. She'd betrayed him by becoming an adult, a potential authority figure ready to join the world in finding fault with him. Once he'd trusted her implicitly but now wondered whose side she was on. He knew. She thought she could manage both him and his father. Rob really disliked anyone trying to manage him.

And the boy. He really liked the kid who seemed to have captured Meagan's lost sense of humor and who looked at him the way his mother once did. Meagan made it clear that Bobby was her first concern. For the first time in his life, Rob understand how his father might have resented the attention his mother had given him. He should have never inserted Meagan into the MacLeod Family Fiasco but he had done what he had done. He couldn't take it back.

Feeling calmer, he wondered how long he could last here. Rob knew the Old Man would never give him enough money to turn this place into an inn and doubted he would ultimately trust Meagan either. The Old Man liked to dangle things like love, money, and promises but always held them just out of reach. Given enough time, he'd ruin the kid too. If Meagan had any sense she'd run back to her parents' house, change the boy's name to Flannigan, and never utter "MacLeod" again.

Rob already felt the urge to drive south but didn't know where to go. His friends were mostly married to women who saw Rob as a threat to the good order and decorum of their unions. He needed a plan. First, he had to survive his parents' visit by not having another blow up with his father or following his mother's old adage, "when times get tough, have a martini." Second, he could hang around here until a real plan came to him. Meanwhile if Meagan reported his every action to his father, he'd see that she regretted it. Her days of hiding in the deep woods with her little bastard were probably over.

♦ ♦ ♦

Rob was relieved to find his mother drinking coffee in the dining room rather than gin in her bedroom. He always liked the dining room wedged between a continuation of the great room's windows and the kitchen. It compressed the great room's grand view of the Lake and sky into a cozy, humane setting. He poured a cup of coffee from the pot on the massive sideboard and sat down beside her.

"Was I terrible last night, Rob?"

"No, Mom, you were fine," Several psychiatrists had told him his relationship with his mother, while loving, was also toxic. In the view of the crazy old men who analyzed others' lives for a living, they were co-dependents. Or had been. Sometimes he thought his mother was too far-gone to know what she was doing.

"Don't let that girl trick you again." She seemed obsessed with Meagan.

"You warned me about her last night. I know what the Old Man is doing. Don't worry about me, I can take care of myself."

After a silence, she muttered "Faded Glory."

"What?"

"Faded Glory. That's the story of my life. That's me. That's us. That's this place. Would you believe I was once the most celebrated debutante in Detroit?"

"I know, Mom. I've seen the photos, remember having the most beautiful mother around. And you are still lovely."

"My father was one of the most respected executives at General Motors, ran all the important divisions. He had great taste, always bought the best for his family. My mother taught me to spend money, make a stiff drink, and write a check. In those days women knew they'd always be taken care of by the men in their lives. Not so different from that girl who lives here. Seduced you so she can live on MacLeod money."

"She isn't living well and she's not so bad." Rob was surprised at his spontaneous defense of Meagan. "In all these years she never asked me for anything."

"That's because your father took care of the situation. Your father was tolerable when he drank but now he's….. I don't know what he is. When he drank he yelled at me but now he just gives me cold, condescending stares and curt commands. I should have married one of the Ford boys. I had plenty of other suitors. Maybe I should have divorced him. I was always waiting for him to divorce me. Your father had a lot of affairs, you know."

"I know but I'd rather not talk about it." He also knew from their screaming bouts that she'd had a fling or two. "Besides, he chose to stay with you."

"What are you going to do, Rob? Your father said something about turning this place into a commercial venture. That's what happens when you live in a state of faded glory." Rob thought Faded Glory would be an appropriate name for the inn that would never happen. "When the past gets monetized, it loses real meaning. I'd hate to see a bunch of strangers sitting at this table, eating off the china I chose for the family."

"Don't worry. It won't happen. It's something for him to dangle in front of Meagan and me. He's just trying to manipulate us. He thinks if he can get me into bed with Meagan, he can use her to control me. Not the first time he's done that. He pushed me to marry Laura because he thought she could manage me. That certainly didn't work."

"I liked Laura. I knew her mother. She had family, not like this girl."

"What the Old Man can't seem to understand is that little Meagan, or any other of the women of his choosing, can't control me whether we're having sex or not. He's dangling marriage in front of Meagan, but you don't have to worry because she doesn't want to marry me. She's not stupid, maybe a little more conniving than I thought, but not stupid. Where are they?"

"Out looking at the property. She called someone; a relative I think. They're making a list of what would have to be done to put the place in order. "

"It was nice of them to include me, especially since it was my idea. Just like the Old Man. I'm beginning to wonder about her."

"That girl looked for you but couldn't find you. Do you think your father is having an affair with her?"

Rob laughed. "You don't have worry about Meagan. She doesn't control men by having sex with them, she does it by not having sex with them."

"I used to like this place but now it's as faded and sad as I am. I hope we leave soon."

"We're all sad, Mom. You're sad, I'm sad, and even the Old Man is sad. What Meagan doesn't realize is if she gets any more involved with any of us, she'll be sad too. That boy still has a chance but not if the Old Man gets a hold of him."

He stood up. "Where are you going?" she asked.

"Now that is a good question. Other people seemed to have a plan for their lives. I wonder why I didn't."

"You didn't need one. Your father had it all planned for you. You'd grow up and take his place as head of the company, head of the family, and the head of the St. Andrew's Society. Same plan his father had for him."

"Trouble with the Old Man's plan was that it didn't work out. He lost the company; probably due to his drinking."

"It wasn't his fault. Who could have known that the American automobile industry would collapse, that cheap parts imported from all those foreign countries would undercut us?"

"Maybe everyone in the auto industry was as drunk as he was. He didn't recognize the company was in trouble until it was too late, and then he didn't do much about it."

"What was he to do?"

"I don't know but he didn't do it. Do you want to go into Marquette for dinner tonight?"

"How can we? We don't have adequate transportation. We can't all get into your little car and that thing she drives is atrocious...and Japanese as well. What is it?"

"A Honda. About fifteen years old, I think."

"Your father will buy her a new car."

"No, he won't. He'll insinuate he will and then never do it. Do you have any idea how much money is really left?"

"He never tells me anything. When my father died, Robert ranted and raved about my father having spent most of his capital and my mother needing the remainder to live on. Your father said any man who goes into his capital is incompetent. Now he's doing the same thing. He just can't stand for his friends to think that he isn't as well off as he used to be. He tries to tell them he closed the company because he didn't need it, but they know better. He's not fooling anyone."

"That's what I thought." Rob started to leave the room.

"Where are you going?" she asked again.

"Back down by the old swimming lake. It's quiet down there. Very meditative…or something."

♦♦♦

Rob tapped his fingers on the dining room table wishing they'd have gone into Marquette in two cars, sparing everyone, especially Bobby, a lecture on the history of the MacLeods. The Old Man began, as he always did, with the wildly beautiful coast of northwestern Scotland and the jewel-like islands jutting out of the turbulent sea. "A land that produced only the hardiest and bravest of men." The Clan descended from Leod who died around 1280 A.D. Leod was the son of Olaf, the Black King of Mann. Rob stopped listening. He'd heard it a hundred times. Even dead drunk, the Old Man could recite the saga of the MacLeods from memory. Leod's two sons fathered the two main branches of the Clan. His branch, hence Bobby's branch, descended from Torquil and was centered on Lewis Island.

During the long list of names and battles that followed, Rob concentrated on Bobby whose bright eyes were fixed on the Old Man. Bobby actually looked interested; as if his brain was soaking up the information. What kind of nine year old was interested in this shit? Rob had been raised on a steady diet of MacLeod mythology. As a child, he thought his ancestors were a race of supermen. Maybe that's why he could never measure up to anyone's expectations: not his teachers, his parents, or his wives. Maybe, not even Meagan's.

Rob was bright but never a good student because of his poor attention span. Similarly, while he had passable skills, he lacked the fortitude to excel at any sports. So, especially after he started drinking alcohol on a daily basis at age fourteen, he fell back on being the wealthy bon-vivant, the amiable rich kid always ready to have a good time. If the money was ever gone, he wondered, who would he be?

He mused that Meagan's polite imitation of listening to the Old Man might be for nothing. Inheritable wealth was relative. What was a lot of money to Meagan was not much to him. He saw Jennie look in from the kitchen and roll her eyes at Rob and her sister. Rob smiled but not a muscle in Meagan's face moved. Rob wasn't sure whether he admired, or hated, her self-control.

One more day, he thought. Then he would drive his parents to Marquette for their flight back to Detroit where they would attend a few parties before returning to the dependable warmth of south Florida. The Old Man had repeatedly commented it would be nice if Bobby and Meagan came to Palm Beach with Rob for Christmas. He wondered if Meagan knew it was a command. He wondered if she would obey it.

By the time the Old Man reached the sixteenth century and Rory Mor MacLeod fighting against the English in Ireland and rebuilding Dunvegan Castle, Rob wondered if he'd overdone Bobby's politeness lessons. His mother pushed her martini glass toward him. He excused himself to get her another drink. He stared at the Scotch. He could taste it. He didn't know how long he could hold out. When he returned to the dining room, the Old Man was promising Bobby a trip to the seat of his ancestry, where they would stay in old castles and visit every island the MacLeods had once ruled.

"Would you like that, young man?"

"Very much, Sir. Of course it is up to my mother."

Meagan smiled. "That would be a wonderful present....perhaps when you graduate from high school. Give you something to work for and look forward to. It would be especially wonderful if three generations of MacLeod men go together. It is very generous of you, Mr. MacLeod." Rob wanted to congratulate Meagan for handing the question. She obviously meant, "probably not" while saying, "it would be lovely." Bobby wouldn't graduate from high school for eight years when, with a little luck, the Old Man would be dead. And she put Rob into the equation, skirting the Old Bastard's attempt to freeze him out of the relationship with Bobby. The Old Man was going to have a harder time with Meagan than he thought.

"Do you know how to do something called Skype?"

"Of course, Sir. I skype with my school friends, especially when we have questions about our homework."

"If I can get someone to set it up on my computer, perhaps we could keep talking about all of these things."

"That would be nice, Sir."

"In the meantime, I will send you some things about the MacLeods." Rob knew the Old Man would send books along with ties and sweaters in the MacLeod yellow and black tartan. He wondered if the Old Man really thought Yooper kids wore matching hand knit ties and sweaters to school, much less in the family tartan. Meagan would undoubtedly take a few photos for the Old Man before packing away the gifts, only to be rediscovered in the far future, probably amid howls of laughter.

Rob wondered if the Old Man would ask questions about Meagan's ancestry. If Rob remembered correctly, her mother was mostly Italian from Hurley, with maybe a Cornish miner mixed in. Her father obviously had some Irish blood, but with a French-Canadian mother who had some Ojibwe ancestors. Meagan would be pure Yooper if she added something Scandinavian, preferably Finnish. But the Old Man didn't ask. He wanted to turn Bobby into a pure MacLeod without reference to his mother.

"Bobby, I think it is time for you to excuse yourself and get ready for bed. You have school and your grandparents have to get ready to leave in the morning."

"Not too early," Rob said. "We'll have to take your car, Meagan. I'll leave you the keys to mine in case you need to go somewhere."

"Oh." They both knew the trip to and from the airport was a little over two hours. He wondered if she suspected he might be a little later than that. "Of course, but I'm not planning on going out."

"Perhaps you should price a new car," the Old Man smiled at her. "The inn will need something more appropriate. Perhaps we could advance that."

"Thank you. Someday. We don't want to spend any unnecessary money at this point. I really appreciate your visit and everything you've done for Bobby. I do hope we see each other sooner rather than later."

Rob smiled. Shit, he thought, she was always one of those lying local people telling us what we wanted to hear. She's still playing games with us. He briefly wondered what she would do if he got into her bed tonight. Would she scream or just play along? He decided he wasn't desperate enough to find out. He saw Jennie half wave at Meagan and then go out the kitchen door to her car. He envisioned the sisters spending tomorrow morning laughing at the MacLeod Family Charade.

CHAPTER 3

Rob knew he wasn't returning right away. He waited until his parents were ready to board the plane before kissing his mother and extending his hand toward his father. He was never sure what kind of response he'd get, but his father reached out to him. "Nice boy you have, shows real promise, and his mother isn't bad either." The Old Man seemed almost effusive that morning. He'd come out of the bedroom in time to see Bobby off to school. "Bring them to Palm Beach for Christmas," he said as they started to board. "We can do a lot with that boy. They might make a man out of you yet."

Rob wondered if his father knew him at all. He lacked the Old Man's easy facility for transforming reality into a world more to his liking. His father seemed to forget that neither one of them had seen "that boy" for over six years which might explain why Bobby was healthy and happy. But Rob didn't want any arguments. He felt euphoric, as if he'd passed some kind of test and now looked forward to a reward he knew he shouldn't have but wanted anyway. He wasn't hurrying back to that big house.

He thought of the Ojibwe Casino but didn't really like gambling. He hated the noise and all of the old people with their walkers and oxygen tanks. Casinos, in Rob's view, were places where losers spent a lot of time and money to realize they were losers. Driving aimlessly around downtown Marquette, he spied a familiar sign on one of the old brick buildings that were the town. His father always liked the Old English Pub at the Lakeside Inn. "A proper place for gentlemen to drink good Scotch," the Old Man declared on a long ago visit. It was the kind of place that made losers feel like winners.

He pulled up to the Inn's main entrance. When no valet appeared, he remembered where he was. "Barbaric," his mother would have said. He found a parking space on the street and headed back to the main entrance. He stopped briefly in the lobby with its dark, wooden paneling and crystal chandeliers before heading into the Pub, where the wood was of a lighter hue and Yooper symbols, such as snowshoes and skis, hung next to bucolic paintings.

He faced the tall, twin stained glass panels that framed the handles of the beer kegs at the center of the bar. Five minutes until noon. Somewhere in the back of his mind he thought if you didn't drink before noon, you weren't an alcoholic. He tried to obey the rule unless, of course, he was on a binge and still drunk from the night before. As a gesture toward decorum, he ordered coffee. And a shot of single malt Scotch.

A waitress delivered a sandwich to a man sitting alone at a table. Rob studied her from behind. Not bad, in her twenties, early thirties at the most. She was about his height, 5 foot 8 inches, although he always added two inches whenever he could get away with it. She was slender with thin, shapely legs that led to generic white tennis shoes. Her straight, black hair, pulled into a ponytail, reached her waist.

She turned, staring directly at him as if she had been aware of him studying her. She wore her green uniform nicely. Meagan had larger breasts but the waitress unbuttoned her blouse provocatively low, suggesting a certain sluttiness that seemed out of place in this imitation of gentility. He liked slutty woman who oozed earthiness. They understood that a good fuck was nothing more than a good fuck.

He smiled and waved her over. "Can I have a hamburger served at the bar?"

"Sure. How would you like it?"

She definitely had some Native-American ancestry. Her skin radiated a barely discernible copper glow and her eyes matched her hair. The bone structure of her face was classic; oval shape and aquiline nose with a slight rise to the cheekbones. He wanted to say he would like her to serve it naked in one of the bedrooms but thought better of it. "I'll have it medium."

"Fries?"

"Why not. It's my day to live dangerously."

He sipped the coffee and then lifted the shot glass. She had the potential of being a strikingly beautiful woman. He wondered what was keeping her in a place like this. The bartender, an older man who looked thoroughly bored, walked down the bar. "She married or anything like that?"

"Paulette? I don't think so, at least not this month. She's got a boyfriend but he comes and goes. Mostly goes. Maybe gone."

"When she returned with the hamburger, he added a $50 tip and handed her his credit card. She gave him a half-cocked smile that seemed to say his intentions were both sleazy and obvious. "Since you're a big spender, would you like some dessert or something?"

"You from around here?"

"My whole life. You a visitor?"

"Semi. My folks have a place about an hour away. Used to spend my summers here."

"Oh, one of those. Are you here long?"

"Depends. What time do you get off work?"

"Been here since six this morning. Get off at two. You sure like good Scotch."

"I'm willing to share."

"I've got customers in the restaurant, honey. I'll check by and see if you want something later."

Honey. He told the bartender to leave the bottle of Scotch. "Hey, she's not a professional or anything, is she?"

"Paulette? She's not adverse to money but she usually just gives it away for free. I'd wish you good luck but you don't need too much with her."

He downed the second shot. Honey. There was something slutty about a woman calling him "honey." It reminded him of his second wife...well almost second wife. He usually told people that he had been married two and a half times because his marriage to Donna Mae ended in an annulment after a mere two months. Actually he didn't remember most of it but was vaguely aware of his mother crying and his father giving his bride a check to sign papers saying that Rob had been too incoherent to enter into a legal marital contract. He still had fond memories of Donna Mae's southern drawl, "but, honey, can't you just do it one more time?"

Paulette didn't hurry back which made Rob wonder if he had misjudged her. Still he was optimistic enough to get a room. Might come in handy if he just passed out. Then at one thirty, she reappeared. "Still want some dessert, honey?"

"Depends. Can you deliver it to my room?" He handed her one of the plastic key cards.

She glanced at it. "Depends. You going to have a fresh bottle of that 18 year old Glenlivet in that room?"

"You can depend on that. Two if you want."

"Then maybe I have a couple of free hours this afternoon."

She was still wearing her uniform when she entered the large corner room painted a crisp white with deep blue floral accents. "Nice room," she commented. Rob knew she really meant it was one of the most expensive. She glanced at the white fireplace filled with birch twigs and colorful leaves. He sat on the bed with a fresh bottle of Glenlivet and two shot glasses on the nightstand.

She stood for a moment with her hands on her hips. "Well, honey, aren't you going to offer me a drink?"

"Sure, let's play a little game. One shot, one piece of clothing."

"Both of us, or just me?"

"I've had a head start. So let's just concentrate on you." He poured a shot and extended it toward her. She laughed and kicked off a shoe. Another shoe, two socks, an apron, a dress, a bra, and a pair of panties later, she was standing in front of him. Eight shots in less than ten minutes. He was impressed. He also knew he wasn't the only one in the room with a serious drinking problem.

"Now what?" He'd already shed his clothing.

He laid back. "Since I'm already hard, just climb aboard."

She collapsed on him less than five minutes later. "Shit, that was fast. You just exploded."

"It's been months. I've been in rehab."

She laughed. "Rehab really worked, didn't it? I was in rehab once. Never going there again. I'd advise you never to go back either, Mr. MacLeod."

"You know my name?"

"You paid by credit card. I have a cousin from over near L'Anse who works in the kitchen. She said your family has a big place, lots of money."

"Is that why you're here?"

"Shit no. I'm here because I like expensive Scotch and can't afford it. You're not bad either but you have to slow down and give a girl a chance to enjoy herself."

A happy sense of warmth enveloped him. His parents were gone, his belly was full of Scotch, and a beautiful woman would undoubtedly spend the night if he so desired. "I think we have a lot in common. You live in Marquette?"

"Yes. I have an apartment, at least for now."

"Planning on moving?"

"Not if I can help it. My roommate left and I can't quite make the rent."

Rob laughed as he reached for the bottle. "You're not too obvious, are you? But, what the shit, I'll bite. How much will you cost me?"

♦♦♦

Rob watched the school bus turning out of the driveway. He waved as it passed. For some inexplicable reason, he wanted to be home when Bobby woke up but was too late. His head hurt. He couldn't understand how Paulette took a quick shower and then went downstairs to work. He hoped Meagan didn't give him a lot of shit.

Her voice came from the kitchen. "Rob, is that you?"

"You expecting anyone else?"

"No, that's why I'm hoping it is you."

She smiled knowingly. "You look terrible. Get some coffee and I'll fix you some breakfast."

He walked into the dining room and cradled his hands around the warm cup. She put bacon, eggs, and toast in front of him and then took a seat across from him. He waited, but she said nothing. "No questions?" he finally asked.

She shook her head. "I have no right to question you. You're free to do whatever you want, whenever you want. I'm just glad you didn't drive home drunk."

"Who said that I was drunk?" She laughed. "Look, Meagan, I don't feel well and don't know what you find so fucking funny. So if you have anything to say, just say it. What do you want from me?"

"What do I want? What we had long ago. We had each other's backs, but you did whatever you wanted and I did what I wanted. No questions, no judgments."

"Sounds like a perfect marriage."

"Sounds like friendship. Sex and commitment introduces things like jealousy and conflict into any relationship."

"Maybe the old friendship thing worked once, but now the Old Bastard is involved. Whose side are you on?"

"Bobby's side."

"Don't be taken in by that Old Fart."

"Knowing your parents explains you better. The only thing I want is to give Bobby a sense of your family without being too involved with your parents."

"And with me?"

Her face softened. "You're his father, Rob. And whatever else you are, you are not a mean person. You can be a very caring man. I want Bobby to know that side of you. I want you to love him. And I want to make something clear. I am not your father's spy or your keeper."

"You're not reporting to him?"

"I'll answer any direct questions honestly, but I have no intentions of volunteering any information. You're a grown man. Whatever you do isn't any of his business either."

He pushed the half eaten food away. "Thanks for the breakfast, Meagan, but I'm really not hungry." He didn't know why because he couldn't remember having dinner last night.

"You need some sleep. My brother-in-law, Jim, is bringing a contractor by this afternoon to look at restoring the boathouse and the party barn. Do you want to talk to them? Shall I wake you up when they come?"

"Why in the shit are you bothering with that?" He was suddenly annoyed. "The Old Man is never going to spend the money. I'm not even sure how much money he really has or how fast he's going through it. He's just promising you things so you will do whatever he wants."

"I'm not stupid. I know everything you say about him is true. But I'm a Yooper. I don't expect the whole loaf, but maybe we can get a few slices. Even if he's stringing us along, if he just fixes the boathouse roof we can decorate the apartment enough to rent it in the summers. If we get another slice, say the party barn roof, we have the makings of an events venue."

"What's this 'we'? I'm not a Yooper. I expect everything served to me at once."

"Well, I was going to say 'I' but thought 'we' sounded better. After all, it is your house and you are entitled to any rents."

"You can keep any rent as far as I'm concerned. If you make improvements, the Old Bastard will probably fire you and refuse to pay the roofing contractor."

"He won't fire me as long as he wants Bobby. He's not the only one who can dangle things."

"Don't do that to that nice little boy." For the first time, Rob realized that he had genuine feelings for Bobby.

"I'd rather live in my parents' basement forever than harm Bobby. I'm not going to let him get too close to your parents."

Rob stood up. "I'm going to bed and don't wake me up. Do you want to take a nap with me?"

She smiled again. "Remember me? I know why you're exhausted. You did not spend the night alone. You have no need for me."

"Swear to God, Meagan, I don't know whether to love you or fear you."

"Time will tell, Rob. Time will tell."

Rob drifted into that state where rationality fades into fantasy. He could see himself in Florida, married to Meagan who never complained about anything, and father to Bobby who looked at him with admiration. Meanwhile, he'd have some slutty woman like Paulette nearby. After the wreckage that was Donna Mae, the Old Man told him never to marry a slutty woman because she'd embarrass him by sleeping with all of his friends. He'd never have to worry about Meagan sleeping with anyone.

♦♦♦

"Dad, do you like the snow?"

The first dozen times Bobby said "Dad," Rob wondered whom the boy was addressing. Rob turned from window where he had been watching snow blow in off the Lake. The bright autumn

64

had turned into a dreary gray as the days grew short. "It's all right. I grew up in Detroit so I'm used to snow. I've been spending more time in Florida and never miss the snow. Would you believe there are people who've never seen snow?"

"How do they know when it's winter?"

Rob smiled. "They don't. Every day can be pretty much the same. Come to think of it, that gets boring too. How was your day at school?"

"All right. I get to do extra math because I'm ahead of my class."

"Then we can't be related. I didn't like school and hated math."

"Dad," he sounded hesitant. "After dinner can you help me with the Lego set you bought for me, you know the one of the Starship Enterprise."

"Sure, Bobby. I'd love to. Good way to spend a snowy night."

"Great. I'll go do my homework now, so we can start right after dinner."

Rob's phone buzzed as the boy disappeared into the sitting room behind the kitchen. Paulette was texting him. *"Hey, how about coming to Marquette so we can get snowed in together? Might be fun."*

He thought about it but decided that he couldn't do that to Bobby. He owed the kid something. *"Can't make it tonight. Have other plans."* Besides, although he'd only known her for three weeks, Paulette was getting clingy. She seemed convinced he was also sleeping with Meagan.

"When?"

"Don't know. Maybe tomorrow. I might meet you at the apartment." He didn't like women who tried to pin him down. He didn't like her apartment either. It was small, cheap, and generally dirty but, since he was paying for it, he might as well use it. Let her guess if and when he was coming, that might make her think twice about bringing other men there.

He walked into the dining room where Meagan was setting the table far too large for three people.

"I heard from your father today. He approved the roofing contract."

"That surprises me. How did you do that?"

"I didn't. Walt, the contractor, did. I called your father while he and Jim were still here. Walt told him the boathouse roof wouldn't survive this winter's snow. In the spring he'd probably have to rebuild the whole structure or tear it down. Told him the party barn might survive one more winter, but it would be cheaper to do while he is already here. We sent him a lot of photos and explanations. I presume your father checked with contractors in Detroit."

"Congratulations. Maybe you'll have your rental next summer."

"I can scrounge some furniture from the house and buy a few things. I can paint when it's not too cold in there."

"If you rent it, will you tell the Old Man?"

"Of course, I'll put the rentals on the books."

"You're too honest."

"No I'm not. If I didn't tell him and he found out, he'd never trust me again. Bobby says you are going to help him after dinner. Thanks."

"For what? The kid will be helping me put the thing together. He's a lot smarter than I ever was."

"He's a good boy."

"Does he ever comment when I'm not here?"

"When you're not here for more than one night, he asks if you've gone back to Detroit or Florida. I tell him 'not yet' because I don't want him to think you will never leave. I say you're visiting old friends in Marquette. Of course I don't tell him your old friend is Paulette Pacquette."

Rob was stunned. "I've never mentioned her name and you've never asked. You are spying on me."

"Rob, this is the U.P. The spaces might be large but people are few and tend to know each other. Jennie heard it from a friend in L'Anse. Paulette's family is from the area. And if I was spying, I wouldn't give it away by mentioning her name."

"I don't want Bobby to know."

"I don't want him to know either. But I can't guarantee he won't hear it from somebody else, even someone at school. It's really hard to keep secrets here. Everyone knows everything about everybody."

"That's scary." He paused. "Do you mean I could go into a bar in Thunder Bay and find out everything you've ever done?"

"Maybe." She smiled. "Maybe I've managed to keep a secret or two. Do you want wine with dinner?"

He nodded. He was trying to control his drinking and avoid the downward spiral he knew would inevitably come. Days of manageable drinking led to binging, but so far only in Marquette with Paulette. He avoided the fact that the binges were growing longer, ending only when he collapsed or got too sick to continue. He ignored what they always told him in rehab; he wouldn't stop drinking until it killed him.

"Bobby," Rob was having trouble concentrating on the Lego pieces. "Do the kids at your school ever talk about me?"

"Not that much. Don't worry, Dad. I'm not the only kid in school whose parents aren't married."

"Does that bother you?"

"No. Mom explained it to me. She said you love each other but don't get married because you'd fight a lot if you did. She told me her father used to fight with her mother and she hated it and doesn't want me to go through the same thing."

Funny, Rob thought. Meagan never told him anything like that. In fact, now that he thought of it, she'd never talked much about herself. He just presumed her family was normal, whatever that meant. "When I was young, your grandparents drank too much and fought all of the time. I hated it too. Your mother loves you very much."

"I know." Bobby looked up at him. "Do you?"

Rob could feel his eyes filling with tears. He remembered desperately wanting his father to love him. "Of course I do." He turned away, embarrassed by his emotions.

♦ ♦ ♦

Paulette was drunk when Rob arrived. "Why aren't you at work?"

"I didn't feel like going. You said you'd be here yesterday." She bordered on belligerent. "Did you bring any decent Scotch?" He'd seen her this way before but only after he too was fully inebriated. For weeks a darker side had been emerging from the good-looking waitress with a taste for expensive Scotch.

Rob didn't like women who got drunk without him. "Be nice, Paulette. You need me more than I need you."

"Oh, you don't think I can find another man to pay my rent?"

"Feel free. You're a beautiful woman but a sloppy drunk. If you fixed yourself up and stayed sober, you could be very successful at getting more than I spend on you. You'd do great in Florida."

"You think your nice baby-mama will go down on you the way I do? You wouldn't be here if she would."

"You don't know what in the fuck you're talking about. Leave Meagan out of it. And you should go to work because you need a job. I'm not about to start paying all of your bills." The irony of his telling anyone to go to work was not lost on him.

"Cheap son-of-a-bitch. You're like all of the other men in the world." He turned to leave. "Hey, where do you think you're going?"

"I don't come here to be abused. I don't even know why I come here."

"I know why; to get high and get laid. All I have is rotgut but it's over there. I know where there's a party. They'll have some interesting stuff. We never go out together. Maybe your woman wouldn't like it."

"She's not my woman."

"Don't leave, honey." Her tone shifted to pleading. "You're right, I need you. Get a drink and lay down. Let me make you feel real good. Real good."

About the time they turned down the third gravel road and onto a rutted snow-packed trail, Rob understood why Paulette had insisted on taking her jeep. He also wondered if this was a good idea. He could feel something sinister bubbling beneath her mood swings. Maybe she was leading him into a robbery or worse. Probably not, he argued with himself. She still needed next month's rent. He took a swig out of the bottle of recently purchased Glenlivet.

He remembered going to Yooper parties at cabins in the woods in his youth. At the time it smacked of danger but was relatively safe. Like the natives, the summer people were relatively few and knew each other. The permanent inhabitants realized their summer friends had parents who could call people in Detroit or Lansing who, in turn, could send an army of state police across the Mackinac Bridge and even influence Yooper judges. It was wiser not to hassle the summer people.

He'd gone to those teenage parties with groups of locals and summer residents. The only time he'd been the sole outsider had been disastrous. It was right after his first divorce. He knew Betsy from the country club. In fact, he'd dated her older sister. Betsy was barely eighteen when she declared her love for Rob and her determination to marry him. Then she announced she was pregnant. Rob's father, who golfed with Betsy's father, insisted upon marriage followed by credible employment.

Initially Betsy had reminded Rob of Meagan in the sense of adoringly approving anything he did. His first shock came the night before their wedding. She objected when he pushed his hand beneath her skirt and into her underpants. Within minutes, he knew why. His motion somehow dislodged her ill-fitted tampon. While he stared at her blood on his hand, she muttered, "Oh, I forgot to tell you. My period started. I'm not pregnant after all."

He was too shocked and too drunk to say anything but "I do" the next morning. The marriage went downhill from there.

Rob didn't mind Betsy leaving him. In fact, he was relieved to see her go along with her list of "ways to fix Rob" and withholding sex to punish his infractions. But he did mind his father screaming about the dishonor he brought to the MacLeods and his mother crying she could never show her face at the country club again. Funny, he thought, the only person who ever cried during all his divorces was his mother.

Since Rob developed the habit of getting even with his wife by leaving her at parties while going off with other women, he didn't get much sympathy from anyone in Grosse Point and environs. So he fled to the U.P. out of season. Left without his usual summer friends, he wandered from saloon to saloon until someone invited him to a party in the woods.

Thoroughly drunk and craving companionship, Rob tried to talk one of the local girls into entertaining him in the back seat of his car. When her boyfriend twisted Rob's arm behind his back and headed him toward the door, Rob either didn't realize or reflect upon the fact that he was the only Troll from the Lower Peninsula at the party. Instead he lost his temper and began shouting obscenities at the locals. He'd never forget his face hitting the gravel driveway because he still had scars on his chin. After being pounded by many people, someone lifted him into the back of a truck. The next thing he remembered was half sitting in the middle of the road in Thunder Bay. His car was parked outside of the nearby Sailor's Saloon.

He couldn't give the Marquette County Sheriff any names and none of the Yoopers remembered the party, much less where it was. All he could say was someone at the bar had invited him to a party. The Sheriff suggested a car might have hit him since he had been sitting in the middle of the road while drunk.

He was still groggy when his father arrived at the hospital. "Damn son-of-a-bitch," the Old Man thundered. "I just paid for your divorce from a nice girl you humiliated over and over again. And now this! I don't know who beat the crap out of you but they saved me the trouble. The doctor says being inebriated probably kept you limp enough to save you from serious injuries. I'm letting the doctor put you in rehab here and when you're finished, you're going to Florida and get a job that you will probably screw up. I don't want you here and I don't want you in Detroit. In fact I don't want you anywhere near me."

When he got out of the hospital, Rob remembered Meagan was living in Marquette. He needed an afternoon of beer and sympathy. But when she opened the door, Meagan threw her arms around him. He still wasn't sure if she cried for him or herself, but by late afternoon they were consoling each other in bed. He stayed for a week, making him late for the job his father had arranged in Miami.

Paulette nearly stumbled as she jumped out of the jeep. An ominous feeling filled Rob as he realized once again he was the only outsider. A scent ranging from ammonia, to paint thinner and to really bad perfume emanated from a shed about ten feet beyond the cabin. He followed Paulette to the snow-encrusted porch where three men drank beer. "Hey Paulette, you brought your Troll sugar-daddy to meet us? Have you heard from your old man lately."

Feeling uncomfortable, Rob debated introducing himself. Paulette intervened. "I don't give a shit about Roy. This one is a lot better. He just wants to have a little fun and has the money to buy it. Got some good stuff inside?"

The one-room structure held a dozen men and no more than five or six women. Rob realized that the "good stuff" included more than meth. In one corner a young man was injecting himself with what looked like heroin while the sweet smell of marijuana drifted across the room.

Suddenly alert, Rob scanned the crowd. Two emaciated men with vacant stares were obviously hopeless addicts. The rest of the men were younger than Rob and in better physical shape; the kind of Yoopers who cut down trees with axes, ran through the woods on snowshoes, and brought down a bear with a single shot. While the group was clearly multi-ethnic, it had a strong Native American presence. The women were a mixed lot, none as good looking as Paulette, but mostly young and not unattractive. Rob had no intention of speaking to any of them.

Rob watched Paulette head for the heroin. Shit, he thought, she had more problems than he had imagined. The man Rob presumed was a dealer, called across the room. "Hey buddy, you good for what she wants?" He moved closer to the dealer who sat on a rickety sofa with some of his wares on a coffee table in front of him.

"Do you take credit cards?"

The dealer, who had a scar across his forehead and tattoos down both well-muscled arms, rolled his eyes, causing Rob to throw a $100 bill on the coffee table. "That will buy more than one hit because I don't do change." He put a tourniquet on Paulette's arm. "What about you?"

Rob considered his options. He was glad he'd left the Scotch in the car because more alcohol could make him more aggressive and he had no doubt what would happen if he got into a fight here. He'd once had a few months acquaintance with heroin in Florida but hated the lows that followed too quickly. He considered meth not only déclassé but injurious to what was left of his good looks. "Do you have any pot?"

The dealer smirked, his dark eyes glimmering with amusement. "A real beginner," he murmured but produced a ten cent bag. "Enjoy. You good for everything Paulette wants?"

"I don't know if anyone is good for everything Paulette wants, but I'm good for whatever she wants tonight."

A tall blond man leaned toward the dealer and whispered.

The dealer laughed. "No, he's all right. He's with Paulette. He's not a narc and if he ever talks about this place, I know where his son lives." The threat sent a chill through Rob. The dealer's face twisted into a wry smile. "Besides, he's almost family. His half-brother was my first cousin. His old man screwed my mom's oldest sister." He looked directly at Rob. "Did you know that?"

Rob didn't know what to say. It wasn't the kind of question people asked around country club bars and pools. "I knew about him but didn't know him. I heard a lot of good things. He must have been quite a guy."

"He was. We grew up together. I loved him like a brother but we had no love for the MacLeods. I always thought I'd slit the throat of any MacLeod I met, but I'll give you a pass for now. Any man who takes on Paulette has to be a little crazy. Now get out of my face before I change my mind. You're holding up my business."

Rob was thoroughly shaken. He knew full well he could disappear forever in these woods and wasn't sure Paulette would even try to help him. He took a chair against a wall and lit a joint. He didn't want any trouble here, even with Paulette. His best bet, he figured, was to keep quiet until Paulette was ready to go. He looked around the room. He thought one guy worked at the gas station in Thunder Bay but he couldn't recall any of the others. He thought he knew the locals, but now realized he only knew the upper echelon. Yoopers who went to parties at summer residences aspired to college educations and lives beyond these forests. They dreamed of leaving the U.P. for lucrative jobs or promising careers. Even Meagan once did. But the people around him felt foreign and decidedly dangerous. Yooper society was more complex than he had imagined.

He watched the dealer out of the corner of his eye. He did not want to stare or ask the myriad of questions running through his mind because he didn't want Bobby to have a dad who died in a meth lab. If his half-brother had survived Afghanistan, would he have come back to this? Would he be the drug dealer who also cooked meth? He grew angry with the Old Man for not giving his half-brother an education, a chance for a better life. Did the Old Man love that boy or did his half-brother stay awake at night, as Rob did, wondering why his father didn't love him. No matter what had or would happen, he didn't want Bobby to suffer as he had.

Rob had just settled into the easy feeling that the rest of the night would go smoothly when he heard a wild wailing. Paulette was face down, pounding the floor with her fists and forehead. All the eyes in the room shifted from her to Rob. He stood up and put a hand on Paulette's shoulder. She looked up and screeched, "Leave me alone, you can't help me, nobody can help me. I should have died. I wish I had died. I want to die."

She suddenly bolted upright and headed toward the door while shedding her clothes. Rob started after her but two of the men on the porch caught her. She flailed wildly as they held her.

Rob could only mutter, "What the fuck?" as half the party spilled out onto the porch.

"She lost the baby three years ago today," a woman muttered.

"She had a miscarriage?"

"No, the baby was over two years old. A pretty little girl. The baby was sick. Instead of taking her to the clinic, Paulette and Roy overdosed on meth. By the time they came to, it was too late."

The drug dealer was at Rob's side. "Get her out of here. I don't want the law nosing around if she manages to kill herself. And don't let her out of the car on this side of Marquette. I don't want anyone finding her frozen body and asking questions. It's a form of suicide up here," he explained, "get a snoot full of booze or drugs and go to sleep in a snow bank or just keep walking into the Lake. Better she's with a rich white man if she kills herself." He saw the shock on Rob's face. "We'll tie her up in blankets and put her in the jeep. You take the crazy bitch wherever you want, just don't bring her back here. That's all you have to do and we'll forget you were ever here. Just don't come back." The dealer started to turn back toward the door but hesitated. "If you have any sense, you'll dump her like Roy did. She's bat-shit crazy."

Soft gray light illuminated the windows by the time Rob drained the bottle of Scotch. If it hadn't been for the GPS on his phone, they'd still be lost in the woods with Paulette alternating between screaming obscenities at being restrained and lamenting her lost child. At least she was quiet by the time they reached Marquette. Rob wondered if any of the neighbors had seen him struggle into the building with Paulette, still tied in the blanket, slung over his shoulder. He'd untied her and put her into bed in case someone called the police.

How could a woman get high rather than taking care of her sick child? He realized he had a double standard, he expected women to behave better than men. One psychiatrist told him he romanticized women and then became irate when they didn't live up to his expectations, especially as caregivers. Rob didn't like the man's suggestions he was angry with his mother for not protecting him from his father. He knew his mother was less than ideal but she had never abandoned him. He started to think she would have cared for him rather than fall into a drunken stupor but stopped short of an answer because he wasn't certain she would.

Paulette. The longer he knew her, the less he liked her. He hadn't thought much about it because she was easily available and sometimes fun. But tonight's revelations were too much. He faced a new truth. She was nothing but a junkie who sold herself for alcohol and drugs and let her child die. He felt absolute disgust but also knew she was the perfect foil for his anger against his family and the world.

He knew he should drink a pot of coffee and drive away from Paulette forever. But he had his own dark side. Where else could he get violently drunk or push a woman around and know it didn't matter…at least to him and his world. He felt the spiral pulling him down, not because he loathed Paulette but because he loathed himself. He'd found a kindred spirit in self-mutilation.

He drove to the Walmart and bought six of the best bottles of Scotch available and then went back to the apartment. He got into bed where Paulette was barely conscious and pulled off her underwear. As he positioned himself over her, he slapped her face. "Wake up you stupid bitch. You've done enough damage for one night, maybe for a lifetime. If that was his baby, Roy should have killed you. I should have let you die in the snow. You're nothing but a hopeless addict and an ignorant whore. I've had a miserable night so now you are going to provide physical relief. God only knows, I paid for it."

She grunted and moved slightly. He pushed her legs apart. He wondered briefly how all those shrinks would rate this as a toxic relationship. He knew it would only get worse; they would claw at each other while trying to escape the prisons of their pasts. The more he'd come to despise her, the more he'd abuse her and had no doubts that she would do the same. It could only end badly.

"Wake up," he slapped her again. She opened her eyes and smiled. Then she lifted her head to spit in his face. "Bitch," he muttered as he pushed into her.

"You weak, sniveling bastard; you prissy little rich boy," she taunted, "you're a poor excuse for a man. I'll bet that woman of yours has a real man on her right now. I'd like a real man like

Roy on me right now." She closed her eyes but played her part in their strange dance of mutual destruction.

CHAPTER 4

"**M**om, does my dad have a girlfriend in Marquette? Someone at school said he lives in Marquette, not here."

"Your dad lives a lot of places. So do your grandparents because rich people have a lot of houses. Sometimes they live here, sometimes in Detroit, sometimes in Florida. So your father can live both here and in Marquette. As far as a girlfriend is concerned, I don't know much about that. Since we're not married I've never asked him. It's none of my business. He can have a girlfriend if he wants. All you have to know is that he is here to see you. If it wasn't for you, he wouldn't be in the U.P. at all."

Bobby seemed only tentatively satisfied with her answer. She had another thought. "When you skype with your grandfather, does he ask questions about your dad?"

"Sometimes."

"What does he ask?"

"He asks where Dad is and what we do together. Sometimes he asks if Dad is sick. I don't know why he asks that."

"What do you tell him?"

"I tell him Dad is fine and plays games with me. I told him how we built a snowman and an icehouse. If I tell him Dad is visiting friends, he asks what friends. I tell him I don't know. Lately I've been lying, telling him Dad is here when he's not. Why doesn't he just talk to Dad?"

"They haven't always gotten along. I don't know the details but your grandfather seems mad at your dad a lot. It is important we do not get in the middle of any fights between them because it won't turn out well for anyone. You don't want either your grandfather or your dad angry with you."

"I like Dad a lot better than Grandpa. Dad is fun but Grandpa is bossy. He keeps telling me we're moving to Florida and I'm going to school there."

"What do you tell him?"

"That it's up to my parents, particularly my mom."

"Maybe it might be better go to high school somewhere else, but I don't think we want to live in Florida. Maybe we could visit Florida sometime, but just for a few days."

"Grandpa keeps saying that we're going to Florida at Christmas."

"I don't think so, Bobby. Your grandfather is an old man. It's important to be polite to him but we really don't have to do what he says. We'll spend Christmas here with my family."

"Will Dad be here for Christmas?"

"I don't know." She was wondering where he'd be for Thanksgiving next week.

Meagan had mixed feelings about Thanksgiving. All of her family and half of Marquette County knew about Rob's increasingly violent affair with Paulette Pacquette. Last week Jennie had come to the house to talk to her about it. Meagan wasn't surprised Paulette's neighbors talked about their loud and often physical battles. They didn't call the police out of fear for the unsavory people who visited Paulette, especially when Rob wasn't around. So, on one hand, Rob's presence at her family's dinner could be awkward. On the other hand, Bobby would be disappointed if he wasn't there.

What had she done? Last September, she'd laughed at Rob when he obviously spent a night with Paulette or whomever. But now she couldn't ignore the fact that Rob was deteriorating. She saw the signs. Rob still came home to recover from his benders, as he called them, but his recoveries were shorter and shakier. She saw his hands tremble and heard him pacing in his bedroom. Thankfully, she had sheltered Bobby to a point where he didn't recognize the sign of deteriorating alcoholism. And the boy adored Rob.

"Mom," Bobby's voice interrupted her thoughts. "I'll ask Dad about Christmas when he comes home for Thanksgiving. "

"If he comes home for Thanksgiving."

"Oh no, he'll be here. He promised me he would."

◆◆◆

When she heard a car coming down the driveway on Tuesday morning before Thanksgiving, she hoped for Rob.

Instead her brother, Don, stepped out of their mother's SUV. "I heard you got in last night," she opened the kitchen door. "Don't you usually go to your in-laws for Thanksgiving?"

He took off his jacket and gloves. "I was in Detroit, so thought I'd fly up. I'll join Fran and the kids in Indiana on Friday."

"Let's have coffee in the dining room. Or would you rather have a drink?"

"A little early to start drinking."

"Really? You've been gone from the U.P. too long. Well, are you here to give me the usual Christmas 'what the shit are you doing with your life' lecture? Am I going to have it twice this year? Mom sent for you, didn't she? She sent for the almighty head of the family to talk some sense into his little sister."

"She's worried about you. And I'm not the head of the family."

Her voice rose. "Yes, you are. You've been the head of the family since you were fourteen years old and nearly killed Pop."

He matched her tone. "Shit, you're difficult. You've always been difficult."

"You mean Jennie and Carol always did whatever you told them but I'm not so good at following your orders."

"They're not any worse for it today. They both have nice husbands and families."

"You mean they have husbands who drink and hunt with you."

"And what do you have? What are you hiding from here? What are you waiting for?"

"I'm waiting for you to stop trying to run my life and everyone else's. You just can't get over the fact I moved here against your wishes….in fact, against your explicit orders."

"I never issued any orders. Are you waiting for that rich lush to get rid of the whore he beats up and make an honest woman out of you? Considering the people she knows, he'll end up disappearing, which might not be a bad thing. God help you if you end up at the end of his fist. I should have killed him when you started hanging out with him. You should find a decent man."

"I'm here," the unexpected voice was weak but steady. Rob was standing in the kitchen door. "You can kill me pretty easily, Don. You are still taller and stronger and I'm a wreck. And you're right; you might be doing everyone a favor. And as far as your sister is concerned, she's the best woman I have ever known...and I don't mean that in the biblical sense. So if I ever abuse her, I'll deserve anything you do to me. I'd marry her in a minute but she's too smart for that. I'm sure my father begged her to marry me. I know she and Bobby are far too good for me. So here I am, Don. Beat the shit out of me if you want."

"How long have you been here?" Meagan asked.

"Not long, just enough to get the drift of the conversation. I was shocked to hear screaming when I walked in the door. I hope Bobby isn't home."

"Of course not, he's at school."

"Good. Then I'll take a shower and a nap. Wake me up before he comes home." He looked at Don. "If you decide to murder me, Meagan will point to my room."

"He looks like hell." Don watched Rob go up the stairs to his bedroom.

"I know. Do you still want coffee?

Don nodded and followed her into the kitchen. "I didn't start out to be head of the family as you put it. I was just a kid protecting our mother from a violent drunk. I was tired of it. Tired of Pop coming home drunk and threatening everyone. You don't remember because you're the youngest"

"I remember rather vividly. I'd hide when he came home from work, or I should say the tavern. You were his favorite punching bag but he was a small man even in his prime. At fourteen, you were a head taller and twenty pounds heavier than he was. He should have known better. Jennie and Carol hid under their beds but I watched. He went for Mom and you yelled at him to stop. He cursed, and said you were next, after he took care of her. So you hit him in the back of the head with a fireplace poker.

Mom cried but you threw cold water on him. When he came around, you picked him up by the collar and told him that his drinking days were over because if he ever came home drunk again or touched any of us, you'd kill him. He must have believed you because I sure did. If he drank after that, he knew not to come home. They'd find him from time to time half frozen in his car or in an alley. Finally, he just gave up and crawled into that easy chair of his."

"You have a good memory. And what happened after I left for college and he came home drunk?"

"I told him I was going to call you and you'd come home and break both his legs so he could never leave the house again. He slept in his car that night too. He doesn't talk about you. Most fathers would brag about a son who runs a large oil refinery in Texas, but he doesn't. Mom does. You're more her God than her son. Pop never expresses an opinion."

"I learned a long time ago to live with the fact that he probably hates me. I just couldn't stand it anymore. I wanted peace, not only for myself but for the rest of you."

They took the coffee into the dining room. "I'm the only person I know who had to ask my big brother's permission to do things, whose mother asked her teenage son for direction. You're more like Pop than you can ever admit. He wanted to impose his sense of order through violence but you imposed yours by sheer force of will. Poor Pop was just a nonentity when you got finished with him."

"He was a nonentity before I threatened him. The only way he could feel important was by getting drunk and threatening his family." He paused. "Does that mess upstairs remind you of Pop? Is that what this is about?"

Meagan smiled. "Rob is more like you than like Pop. He hates his father and tries to protect his mother, except his mother is a lush too. And if Bobby ever hits him over the head, Rob will get up swinging. Pop learned to take orders from you, but Rob is stuck in teenage rebellion. Telling him what to do is a guarantee he won't do it."

"Do you think you are in love with him? Is that why you've been hanging around here all these years?"

"Maybe I love him a little, but I'm not in love with him. I never was."

"I'd like to think you were when he seduced you?"

"He didn't seduce me. I initiated it."

"Nobody likes to hear their little sister say that."

"It's true. I was having boyfriend troubles. Todd had just told me he was getting married."

"And that upset you? I know you went steady with him for a couple of winters but Todd Leino? You really have strange tastes in men; glib Rob in his sports cars during the summers and mute Todd in his old truck during the winters. Did Todd ever talk to you? He never talked around anyone else. What could you have seen in him?"

"You forget, he was the high school basketball star. That comes with some glamour. He was even taller than you. And we did communicate in a way. Nobody likes to have an old boyfriend, or girlfriend, stop by to say 'Hey, I've found someone I like better than you.'"

"Doesn't seem like a good reason to jump in bed with that drunk."

"School wasn't going well either."

"You always had good grades. You shouldn't have quit. Other women with children go to school."

"It wasn't just grades. I felt out of place."

"You were only an hour away at Northern Michigan in Marquette. You really don't make any sense."

"Whatever. I just wanted to take care of Bobby and the MacLeods gave me a way to do it."

"I still think Bobby is your excuse for hiding here. I've told you a million times. If you move to Houston, I'll find you an office job in the refinery, and you'll have instant family. Bobby has cousins in Houston too."

"I've always planned to leave here when Bobby goes to college. Maybe when he goes to high school. Maybe he should go to high school somewhere else. This place is too inbred. Everyone knows too much. Bobby isn't going to hear nice things about his father. I should start taking some college courses, maybe online."

"I hear Old Man MacLeod is taking an interest in Bobby. You haven't been hanging around here hoping Bobby will inherit some money?"

"When I was young, I envied the summer kids. I thought they had perfect, happy lives. I wanted to live in a big house and now I do…. Don't say it. I know I'm a glorified servant…. But now I realize these big houses are falling apart. I wanted to have a lot of money but now I've seen what money has done to Rob and his parents. My goal for the MacLeod money is to have them pay Bobby's tuition. I want him to go someplace other than Northern Michigan. I want to get him out of the U.P. I want him to have a good start in life."

"I started out at Northern Michigan and have done all right. Bobby doesn't have to go to Harvard to have a good life."

"I want him to have a father too. Since he's been here, Rob has been good to him."

"You mean when he's not getting drunk with that slut in Marquette."

"I want you do to a favor for me. Rob is here because he promised Bobby he'd be at Thanksgiving dinner. For Bobby's sake, don't let anyone belittle Rob or argue with him. Don't insist he drinks. Let Bobby have his daddy at dinner just once. Please, Don. If you're nice to Rob, everyone else will be too."

Don stood to leave. "All right. For you and Bobby. I'll tell Mom you are as stubborn as ever but you don't exhibit any signs being abused. Did he really ask you to marry him?"

"That's the strange part. His father wants him to marry me and he agreed. Of course, who knows if he would actually show up for the ceremony? Probably would. He's used to getting married. I think I'd be wife #4 and he isn't even thirty-five years old. At this point, I just feel is sorry for him."

"All right," Don put on his jacket and gloves. "When you move to Houston, we'll find a good high school for Bobby. And don't worry about the MacLeods. I'll pay Bobby's tuition. Maybe you can contribute when you get on your feet financially."

Meagan shook her head as Don drove the SUV into the falling snow. "Just like you, Don," she murmured to no one in particular. "Not asking if I want to move to Houston but telling me what will happen when I move to Houston. There's no way I'm ever moving to Houston and back under your thumb."

♦♦♦

Meagan thanked Don for his cooperation as they left the Flannigan house. She thought things went well. Once when Rob's hand started to tremble, she covered it with hers. Toward the end of the evening, he'd had two beers just to be social, he said. Now back in the sports car heading out of Thunder Bay where Meagan's father had once owned the gas station and then managed the long-gone grocery store, Bobby seemed especially happy. "That was fun, Dad. I hope you'll still be here at Christmas."

"I hope so too. But sooner or later, I'll have to go to Florida."

"Grandpa MacLeod says we're all going there right after Christmas."

"Grandpa MacLeod says a lot of things. Don't pay any attention to him. The only person you really should pay attention to is your mother. Always do what she tells you because she will always have your best interests at heart."

"Don't you, Dad?"

"Yes, I want to do what is best for you, but your mother is a lot stronger than I am. She's a wonderful person."

"That's enough," Meagan laughed. "Don't lay it on so thick."

"I have a lot of weaknesses," Rob continued. "Someday I'm afraid you'll find out and not love me anymore."

"I'll always love you, Dad."

"I honestly think you might."

Once Bobby was in bed, Meagan could hear Rob in the great room. She stood in the doorway and watched him pour Scotch into a glass. "I have to go back to Marquette."

"You don't have to go. Especially not tonight, the snow is getting thicker. You could get caught in a white-out."

"Is there ever a time when it isn't snowing up here? I thought Detroit was bad. Now I understand the Lake Superior

Snow Machine. It picks up moisture over the Lake and dumps it all on the U.P."

"It's a long holiday weekend and Bobby will be disappointed if you aren't here in the morning. Can't you stay a day or two longer?"

"I knew it was only a matter of time before you started telling me what to do."

"I'm not telling you what to do, I'm begging you. Is there anything I can do to make you stay longer?"

"And now the righteous nobility. 'Kind sir, I will sacrifice my virtue if you will only help this poor child.' Really, Meagan, you can do better than that."

"What's wrong with you, Rob? Can't you do this for your son?"

"I am. I don't want Bobby to remember me as a falling down drunk, much less a mean one."

"You weren't a mean drunk when we were young."

"I hid it better then. It's gotten harder with age. Or maybe I just don't care anymore."

"All right, do whatever you have to do." She turned to go back to her bedroom.

"Come upstairs with me." She looked at him. "It's not what you think. Just come upstairs."

Once in his bedroom, he opened a window. "What are you doing? It's freezing out there."

"I don't want Bobby to smell the smoke. As I recall you used to smoke a little pot. I remember sharing more than one joint with you." He reached into a nightstand drawer. They settled on the window seat with a stream of cold air hitting their faces so they could blow smoke out of the window. After taking an initial drag, he handed it to her. "There's something strange about your family."

"No shit. There's something strange about everyone's family. Would you believe I once thought you had an idyllic family life?"

"Your father doesn't say anything. He just sits there while everyone treats your brother like a king."

"He is." She took another drag. "Let's just say my father and Don once had an argument about who was going to run things and Don won."

"I have to admire Don for that. I should have been hanging out with him instead of you. I might have learned something."

"You're not Don. He thinks he's born to rule. Had a great moral sense where his little sisters were concerned. Always preaching at us about how to behave and warning us against boys. I don't know what he was doing sexually, but he wasn't expecting us to do anything. I wasn't the first to get pregnant. Jennie was pregnant but Jim married her before Don found out. Don had a fit when he found out I was about to be an unwed mother. As my punishment I would live at home and drive to class at Northern Michigan, while Mom took care of the baby. Then I'd get a job in the area, so Mom could keep watching the baby and reporting my activities to him.

"You didn't tell me any of that."

"I didn't want Don running my life. I didn't want a marriage based on 'you have to'. When your father's lawyer showed up, Don was in Ann Arbor but Mom called him. Don laid out his plan for my future, which included a large cash settlement from your family in return for my signing away any future claims on them. I followed the lawyer out to his car. He called your father on his phone and we worked out the arrangement and signed it before Don got home. I moved out of my parents' house before they knew about my salary, or allowance, or whatever you want to call it. But I didn't give up Bobby's claim to anything. We really had a screaming match when Don showed up here. I was afraid he'd physically force me to go back home but, I guess, he realized he couldn't keep me there and couldn't undo the agreement."

"You should have told me.

"Why? What could you have done? Don was my problem, not yours. I know he means well but he thinks he has all the answers. He's still making plans to salvage his wayward sister's life."

"I think he's met his match. You always did pretty much what you wanted."

"This place became my refuge, a place of escape. Don keeps referring to it as my prison, but it's really my freedom."

"Maybe he's right. Maybe you should find yourself a decent man."

"I sometimes think 'decent man' is an oxymoron." They both took another drag. "It's your turn to be honest. Tell me about Paulette. Are you serious about her?"

"Sure I'm serious about her. I'd seriously like to wring her neck. If I really want to horrify the Old Man, I'll marry Paulette and take her to his clubs."

Meagan sat straight up. "You're thinking about marrying her?"

"I'm not that crazy. No, I'm not going to marry her; she makes my second wife look like a Vestal Virgin. And I'm pretty sure Donna Mae was a professional. I don't plan on getting married again. Of course, the Old Man keeps trying. You're not the first woman he recruited to marry me. Did I ever tell you about my last wife, Laura?"

"No, we haven't talked like this for years."

"That's a shame because I always felt better after talking to you."

"So what about the last wife?"

"After a perfectly inappropriate but brief marriage to Donna Mae, the Old Bastard decided I needed a keeper. So he settled on Laura. He knew her family from his Florida country club and she was...maybe still is... a Ph.D. candidate in psychology. The perfect caretaker for crazy old Rob. And she was getting desperate. She certainly wasn't the most attractive woman I've ever met. Not that she was grotesque or anything. God knows, most women can be attractive given time and money. She has a long face and big ears that reminded me of an old hound in the cold light of morning. She pretty much camouflaged her flaws with long hair. She spent an enormous amount of time at her hairdresser's because her hair was naturally thin. Or maybe she was paying her hairdresser to fuck her. She never smiled. That's what really made her unattractive. And she was closing in on forty years of age. Guess the Old Man thought I needed a more mature woman."

"I can just imagine my concerned father complaining to Laura about his screwed up son. Maybe she volunteered to help. Anyway, Laura and her family started showing up everywhere I went. My parents invited them to the house so often, I thought they'd moved in."

He lit a second joint and passed it to Meagan. "Laura kept inviting me to her apartment but I always made excuses. When I got home one night, Laura was having coffee and brandy with my parents. I presumed her parents had left earlier. I made excuses for not showing up for dinner and went to bed. Before long this lanky, bony, naked body was rubbing up against me. I didn't want to be impolite and not give her what she was expecting. It was a little embarrassing in the morning. She asked me to go to a play with her, some tickets she'd bought at a charity auction. What could I say? We ended up at her place which was lovely." He laughed. "I should have asked for that apartment in the divorce settlement. It was the only good thing about her. Anyway, I went on a bender and a couple of nights later woke up to hear her telling one person after another that we were engaged."

"Why didn't you tell her that you weren't engaged?"

"I tried but she cried. I hoped a long engagement would show her how boorish I can be. But she and my parents must have had the whole wedding planned because within two months, I went to a very large wedding. To my shock, it was mine. I got so drunk on our wedding night I couldn't do my husbandly duty. In fact, after she announced our engagement, she pretty much turned me off."

"The next morning, instead of being pissed about the wedding night, she began analyzing why. Her favorite hypothesis was that I'm commitment phobic, which is probably true. Within weeks I couldn't stand her. She analyzed everything I did. If I spilled a drink, there had to be a reason. If I liked a movie, it had to have a meaning. She followed me around. I felt like the subject of some fucking experiment. She wanted a baby and she wanted it now. I later learned my father offered her half a million dollars if she got pregnant. I don't know why. Her father is one of those geeky hedge fund guys from New York who has a lot more money than my Old Man."

He passed the joint to Meagan who shook her head. "Bobby will get me up early."

"I started blatantly going out with other women, which got me out of my first marriage. She'd just take my hand and say 'we have to get to the bottom of this behavior.' I told her the marriage just wasn't working out. She told me I wasn't giving it enough time; that I'd grow into it. I argued we were mismatched. She argued we wouldn't know until she helped me 'progress into a more adult state.' I packed my bags and rented an apartment. My parents reverted to their habitual behavior; Mom cried and the Old Man screamed." He put his arm around her. "Do you mind if I close this window?"

"No, close it. I presume Laura got the idea after you moved out." She put her head on his shoulder, her eyes closing.

"She was…maybe is… the most persistent human being I have ever encountered. She started showing up at my place asking when I was returning to her apartment. She started stalking me. Nothing seemed to faze her. Maybe she liked being humiliated, but I think she was just desperate for a husband and a family. That, and I believe, I was fodder for an article in some learned journal if not the subject of a doctoral dissertation. One night I was having dinner in a restaurant with another woman when Laura arrived alone. She quietly sat down at our table and began explaining to my date that I had certain mental problems but that she was working on them. I snapped. I just went wild. I dumped my dinner on her head and then knocked over the table. In fact, I kept knocking over tables. Had about half of them on the floor and the other diners cowering in corners by the time the police arrived. I was yelling she was nuts but I guess the police thought I was the crazy one. But it worked. I had to end up in a mental ward, but she finally filed for divorce.'

"That would be funny if it was in a movie."

"I just figured out why I've always liked you. You've always treated me like I'm a serious human being, not just some kind of a screwed-up mental case. And you are a great mother."

"You're really messed up, Rob, but you're not crazy."

When she awoke, her head was still on his shoulder and his arm still around her. She shook him gently, "Rob, wake up and go to bed. I'm going downstairs." His eyes flickered for a moment, "Sure." She didn't wait to see if he did. But he stayed until Sunday afternoon.

♦ ♦ ♦

Meagan looked twice at her phone. Rob never called her. He checked in with Bobby, asking about his day at school and making small talk. "Meagan," his voice sounded strange. "Help me."

"Help you with what?"

"I'm sick."

"Sick or drunk?"

"I was drunk but now I'm sick."

"Where are you?"

"Paulette's apartment."

"Where is she?"

"On the floor."

"What is she doing on the floor?"

"I don't know. Probably passed out. Maybe dead."

"My God, call 911! I'll call 911!"

"No, you come, I need you to come."

"What's her address?"

"I don't know."

"I'll look it up on my phone. I'm leaving now. This better not be some kind of joke."

Meagan called Jennie as she pulled around the snow bank at the end of the driveway and asked her to pick up Bobby at school and take him to her house. Midway to Marquette she called Rob's phone but he didn't answer. If this turned out to be some kind of drunken hoax, she'd kill him.

She knew she had found the right four-family apartment building because Rob's red sports car was conspicuously outside. Not the kind of building she expected a MacLeod to frequent. She knocked. No answer. She knocked again and thought she heard a muffled cry. She turned the doorknob to no avail. Then she threw her weight against the door and nearly fell into the room. Really cheap lock, she thought. The minute she was inside, she knew why Rob didn't wanted her to call 911. Empty liquor bottles and discarded needles and syringes were all over the place. "Must have been some party," she murmured. She stepped into the small kitchen filled with half eaten food, and dirty dishes. The floor was so filthy it stuck to her shoes. She didn't look too hard for fear of finding various kinds of vermin.

She found them partially clad in the bedroom, Rob moaning on the bed and Paulette face down on the floor. She stepped over Paulette to touch Rob. "Oh fuck, you really have a fever." He looked up at her, his eyes having trouble focusing. "I'm going to call 911," she said.

"No, just take me to Marquette General. I have this terrible pain in my back and keep having hallucinations. Get my clothes over there. Take me to the hospital."

Meagan reached down to be sure that Paulette was breathing. She stirred, "fucking bastard," and then collapsed back into a silent heap. "We can't leave her here, Rob."

"Take me to the hospital and then call the police or her friends or something."

"Why is her face so bruised?"

"I hit her. She came at me with a knife."

"Nice games you two play." As he pulled himself up she noticed human claw marks on his face and dry blood covering a wound on his shoulder. "It's a wonder you haven't killed each other."

"Please Meagan. Get a trash bag and pick up anything that looks like it belongs to me." Instead, she helped him dress. Then she shoved his wallet and phone into her purse and put his keys in her pocket. She half carried him to his car. Once he was inside, she moved her car to the next block and ran back to Rob's.

The nurse took one look at Rob and sent him to an examination room. Realizing for the first time that she was shaking, Meagan sat down to provide information for hospital admissions. When asked her relationship, she simply said, "I'm an employee of the family. He called me to say he was sick, that he'd pulled over to the side of the road and needed help."

She sat nervously in the waiting room wondering how to help Paulette. A doctor appeared. "I understand you're not related."

"No."

"Does he have any family here?"

"No, his parents are in Florida. I look after their estate just on the other side of Thunder Bay."

"It's a good thing you found him. He has a very advanced case of pneumonia. Right now his condition is precarious. We're running blood tests but maybe you can save us some time. Does he, to your knowledge, have a drug or alcohol problem?"

"All of the above."

"We thought so. We've started an antibiotic drip and will move him into the Intensive Care Unit. Who will be responsible for his care?"

"He comes from wealthy summer people. I'll call his father. He'll send somebody. I have to run to Walmart but I'll be right back."

She paid cash for a prepaid phone, reported a break in at Paulette's apartment, and then threw it away. On the way back to the hospital she called Jennie who let her talk to Bobby. She explained his dad had pneumonia and was in the hospital. She was going to stay in Marquette overnight to be certain that he was all right. She'd call him in the morning. While waiting for Rob to be moved into Intensive Care, she called Mr. MacLeod. He cursed at her for not telling him about Paulette, and then said he'd have his local lawyer come by the hospital to see how much trouble Rob was in this time. Meagan wondered if her days at the MacLeod Place were about to end.

Since he had no one else, the hospital let her sit with Rob throughout the night. She held his hand and wanted to cry, not so much for his illness as the way he'd screwed up his life. In the morning, the lawyer who had drawn up the settlement when Bobby was born appeared. "Well," he said, "if I'm going to take care of this, you'd better tell me everything. I find the chapel is a good place to talk. Nobody ever bothers you there."

"Do you think anyone saw you at the apartment?" he asked when she finished her story.

"Probably."

"Well, I'll check on the Pacquette woman. She's probably in detox. I don't think she'll talk to the police. Her acquaintances are not inclined to include the law in their discussions. A little money will go a long way with her. Young Mr. MacLeod might have more to worry about from her friends than from the local police."

"Thank you."

"You don't look so good. Get a motel room. I'll pay for it and put it on Mr. MacLeod's bill."

"But I can't stay here. I have a child."

"Yes, I recall. Don't you have family to look after him? The elder Mr. MacLeod would like you to stay here until you can take his son home. He doesn't trust his son not to leave or say unfortunate things. Mr. MacLeod thinks you have a calming effect on his son." He paused. "Rob MacLeod is a very sick man. He needs encouragement to live."

Meagan spent three nights in Marquette. When Rob left Intensive Care for a regular room, she drove to Jennie's to assure Bobby that Rob would be all right. Then she drove between the hospital and Jennie's house until she took Rob home.

Jennie and Bobby met them at the door. Rob hugged Bobby who told him they had prepared the big downstairs bedroom so they could be closer if he called them. Jennie left, Meagan prepared dinner, and Bobby talked to his father. When Meagan brought Rob his medicine, Bobby went to do his homework. "What would I have done without you, Meagan?"

"You'd have probably have called 911 or somebody else."

"Why do I always do such shitty things to you? You've never been anything but good to me. When I woke up in Intensive Care, I thought you were an angel."

"You were delirious from the fever. And you don't do shitty things to me. After all, you gave me a wonderful son."

"No," he said. "I do shitty things to you. And you're probably the best person I know."

◆◆◆

A week later Meagan rolled a cart down the dairy aisle of Walmart when Gary Guthrie approach her. "Aren't you MacLeod's girlfriend?"

"I'm only an employee."

"Do all his employees have his kid?"

"What do you want?"

"How is he?"

"Still weak. He spent a week in the hospital. I won't ask how you know him."

"Do you remember me?"

"I know who you are. You went to school with my brother."

"We played football together; first against each other and then on the same team. It was a lot easier playing on the same team. I always liked Don. So maybe I like you too."

"What are you trying to say?"

"You know about Paulette Pacquette?"

"Who doesn't?"

"Did you call the police?"

"Why?"

"A woman called. I figure it was you. Maybe you saved Paulette's life. Maybe you sent her to jail. MacLeod's lawyer sort of volunteered to represent her on the drug charges, so she probably won't serve much time, if any. But some of her relatives think MacLeod should suffer if she does. It's all talk at this point and probably nothing will happen. But if I was MacLeod, I'd go where all the rich people go in the winter."

"And what about me? Should I leave too?"

"You don't have to. I'll see no one bothers you or the kid. Like I said, I always liked your brother. He knew how to treat people. I hear he's done well in the big, bad corporate world, but we knew he would. He's smart and knows how to organize. If he'd stayed here, I'd probably be working for him now."

Meagan wasn't about to ask 'doing what' although the remark shed interesting light on Don. "Thanks for the warning. I'll pass it on to Rob."

"And tell your rich bastard friend he owes me big."

Meagan sat on Rob's bed once Bobby left for school. "Gary Guthrie? Is he a big guy with short dark hair and a scar on his forehead? I just knew him as the dealer. Interesting he sent a warning because I have no idea why. He warned me about Paulette too. I should have listened to him. I want you and Bobby to come with me. I don't want to leave you here holding the bag. I have some income, so I can provide, not lavishly of course."

"No, taking Bobby out of school suddenly would be too confusing for him. I think we'll be safe. I'll have to call my dear brother and ask about his relationship with Gary. Now that I think about it, my parents never questioned Don. If he didn't talk Mom into turning the family finances over to him, he at least had a say in everything. Don not only paid our tuition at Northern Michigan but his at Ann Arbor. He had a lot of summer jobs but still..."

Rob smiled. "Do you think your teenage brother was the Yooper version of the Godfather? You're making too much of this. Maybe Don just got Gary out of trouble or backed him in a fight. I thought your brother was a straight arrow."

"In a way. Mom always lectured us about what the neighbors would think. Don did too. We had to keep a certain public decorum even though everyone knew the truth. You don't understand small towns. We used to call you summer people snobby but small towns are snobbier than big cities. In Detroit, you don't know any poor people and poor people don't know you, unless they work in your houses. The rich and poor know the other exists but don't face each other on a daily basis. You only associate with your own kind."

"You snowbirds might be the upper class during the summers, but we have our own a class system during the winters too. Once the mine proprietors, logging company owners, and ore boat captains were the upper class but they either moved away or slipped down the ladder. In fact the whole social ladder slipped down several economic rungs once the easy copper and big trees were gone. Now small business owners are the best we have, followed by those with steady white-collar jobs. When Pop owned the gas station, my mother belonged to a very exclusive bridge club of only four members. They debated whether the school teachers were good enough to join. They decided against it because teachers had to work during the afternoons when they were free to play cards."

"Seasonal manual labor, like loggers, followed by the habitual unemployed who scrounge for living any way they can, form the lower classes. Not only does everybody know where everyone else stands on the social scale, but where their grandparents did. Unlike the big city, we see each other every day; in schools, churches, taverns, and diners. The business owner might exchange pleasantries with the likes of Gary Guthrie but everyone, including Gary, knows the business owner will never, ever invite Gary to his house. The economic differences are wider in the cities, but more personal in small towns, more in-your-face. Sometimes it's stifling. That's why I want to get Bobby out of here for college, and maybe even high school."

"I never thought of it that way."

"So there we were, the Flannigans, slipping down from proprietary class. I reacted by trying to pretend, at least for the three months every year, that I was summer royalty. Meanwhile Don looked downward for support. He had a lot of friends like Gary Guthrie as well as some who met Mom's approval. So now I'm asking myself what Don was really doing."

"Meagan, maybe you brother dealt some drugs but he didn't get rich doing it. There isn't much more than survival money in places like this, even in big cities unless you're a big wholesaler with a good distribution system. If there was any real drug money here and Don was into dealing, he'd probably still be here. He was smart enough to know the real money is in corporate America. Those who run it would milk it dry if they could, and some do. Just look at what happened in 2008. Your brother probably wasn't even dealer level if he was anything. He was smart enough to know where the real money is."

"Rob, I hope we can always be friends. When you first showed up here, I wasn't sure but I want us to always be friends."

He looked away. "I don't know if that's possible. I'll call my father and see about going to Florida. In a week I'll drive to Detroit and fly from there."

♦ ♦ ♦

Meagan wiped tears from her cheeks as Rob got ready to leave. He hugged Bobby, gripping him tightly. "Hey, be good for your mother. Take care of her. I want you to remember I love you, no matter what happens or what anyone ever says. You'll always be my boy. I may not be the most dependable guy in the world, but I'll always help you if I can, no matter what happens. Now go to school and make me proud of you."

Rob started crying as Bobby clung to him. "Go on, now. I have to go to Florida to finish getting well. You have to be the man of the house. The bus will be here soon. I'll call you tonight. Now go on."

They watched Bobby walk down the driveway and onto the school bus. "He's a great kid. I never expected to feel this way about him."

"Of course you would. He's your son."

"I honestly wish he was."

"What are you talking about? Of course he's your son. I have a DNA test to prove it."

"When I was hallucinating in the hospital, I knew I had to tell you. It was all I could think about. I ordered the DNA test and got the results. I didn't like the results so I bribed the technician to change them. He destroyed the sample and raw analysis and rewrote the summary. Bobby is not my biological son."

She stared at him as the initially unintelligible words took root in her brain. "You're joking. This can't be true. This is crazy. This can't be happening. Why would you do something like that? It doesn't make any sense."

His voice wavered. "When Betsy wasn't pregnant after the first year, she insisted on tests. My sperm count is really low. Not impossible but improbable. The Old Man started making snide remarks about my manhood. When I told him you were pregnant, he said I didn't have it in me. I wanted to prove him wrong."

She shook with rage. "You really did do this," she screamed. "You did this because of your eternal fight with your father? Men and their fathers! My God, you've ruined my little boy's life because you didn't like what your father said to you! I don't believe this. I wish I'd let you die in that whore's bed. I've never wanted to kill anyone before but I want to kill you now. Do you realize what you've done? Your father will probably throw us out of here and I'll have to crawl to Don just to feed Bobby. We'll have to leave here forever because Bobby will be a laughing stock. You son-of-a-bitch, you just told a little boy you loved him and now you're going to destroy him. How am I ever going to explain this to him? He'll be devastated."

Rob's voice rose to match hers. "And who is the father, Meagan? Did you really think I was the father? Or was my father right? Was it all about money?"

"I thought you were the father because you were the last person I had sex with before I found out I was pregnant. And when I asked you about a condom, you said we didn't need a condom because you'd taken care of that problem. Later I figured you'd lied to me."

"Who was he? There must have been somebody else around. Think about it, Meagan."

She stared at him blankly for a moment. "There wasn't one, there were two. And they both used condoms."

"Two? Sweet little Meagan Flannigan was sleeping with three men at the same time?"

Her face flushed with raw anger. "Don't you dare give me that kind of attitude! How dare you! You, who I rescued from death's door. You, who I found half naked with a woman who just stabbed you. You, who probably deserved it for beating her up. You, who can't control any of your appetites. You have no right to lecture me about anything. Now get out of here before I get my gun and shoot you. And I won't just graze your shoulder."

He grabbed her and pushed her against the wall. She could feel him shaking too, tears still rolling down his face. "I'm not proud of what I did. And if I hadn't, where would you be now? Would the other guys have seen that you had a place to live and enough money to stay home with Bobby? I don't know who they are, and I'm not sure I want to know, because neither of them is good enough to be Bobby's father. If you want Bobby to be a MacLeod, let him be a MacLeod. Only three people know about this. You, me, and the technician. I've never told anyone. And I don't think the technician will either."

"I know you. You'll let your father get fond of Bobby and then you'll tell him, just to spite him for whatever you think he did to you. You don't care about anybody but yourself. You betray everyone who tries to love you."

His hands dug into her shoulders. "No I won't. When I looked into Bobby's eyes I saw myself at his age. I remembered how it felt to be unloved. He may not be my biological son, but he's the closest thing I'll ever have to a son. He's the one person on this earth I don't think I'll ever want to hurt."

"I wish I could believe you. I'll never believe anything you say again. I'm so confused. What do I do now? The whole life I planned for Bobby just evaporated. And let me go. You're hurting me."

His fingers bruised her shoulders "I know this is another shitty thing to do to you, but the decision is yours. You decide. If you want to find the biological father and acknowledge him, I'll be devastated. If you want to forget this conversation and keep Bobby as my legal heir, I'll do everything I can to help you."

"You could have other children. What then?"

"I'd feel sorry for any children I'd have because they won't have you for a mother. They would just have me and some whore like Paulette or a nut case like Laura. I don't plan on having children."

"God, Rob. How can you have done this to me? What if Bobby takes another DNA test for some reason? What am I going to do?"

"That's one of the reasons I told you. I wanted to prepare you." He finally released her as his voice returned to normal. "Don't do anything right away, especially don't tell Bobby without thinking it through. It's our secret. Take your time. I know you don't believe this, but I will do anything to help him."

"Get out of here. Go to Florida or Hell or wherever. Just leave because I'm still thinking about how much I'd enjoy putting a bullet through your head. The only thing stopping me is Bobby would be parentless if I did. Just leave."

"I'll text you later."

"Don't bother."

"I think I love you, Meagan."

"I know I hate you, Rob."

Meagan's red-hot fury turned to mind-numbing anguish when, by late afternoon, the company that did Bobby's DNA test confirmed, via email, Bobby's file only contained the final report. They could not explain what happened to the raw data or preliminary findings. Meagan slumped into a chair. Rob wasn't lying, just trying to upset her for some weird reason. It was true. Her world, plans, and hopes twisted into unfathomable, unfocused shapes.

Citing stomach problems, she told Bobby she just wasn't feeling well. She managed to put dinner on the table before turning on the television and sinking into her end of the sofa.

"Mom, I just skyped with Dad," Bobby said sometime later. "He's in Detroit. He said to tell you he's sorry. Why is he sorry?"

"I don't know."

Bobby sat on the sofa and hugged her. "Don't cry, Mom. You keep crying when you think I'm not looking. I know you miss Dad. I do too."

"Go to bed, Bobby. I'm going to watch for a while." She had no idea what was on the television screen. All she could think of was what she was going to tell Bobby and how it might affect the rest of his life.

CHAPTER 5

In the days that followed, Meagan increasingly felt one with the frozen landscape. Snow overwhelmed the northwestern side of the house just as Rob's revelation overwhelmed her. The great inertia of heavy, sinking, frigid air penetrated her soul. She couldn't move or think, much less act. She felt trapped, imprisoned by events she couldn't fix and didn't understand. In such an environment, she could barely breathe much less form a coherent thought. Time and place solidified into one great, unmoving mass.

Jim was coming in the afternoon to shovel more snow from the roof but now she envisioned the whole edifice collapsing on her, just as her whole world collapsed with Rob's words. She pulled the collar of her winter coat closer to her chin. She should be in the little sitting room where it was warm but she just couldn't leave the great room with its shrinking views of the Lake. Like her world, drifts of hazy, white snow increasingly obscured any path ahead.

She forced herself to go through the motions of cleaning up about an hour before Bobby came home from school every day. She struggled to hold herself together through dinner but then spent hours in front of the television although her mind was blank. She'd have to move earlier today. She knew her family was concerned about her and, if she didn't appear somewhat like her old self, Jim would report the fact to Jennie. Even Bobby was looking at her with concern.

She found herself looking at Bobby in a different way. She searched his face, his manner, and his movements for signs of the men who had shared her bed in the days before Rob came to her door. Everyone always said Bobby looked like her. He did. He had the same coloring, the same round face, and the same wide smile. Once she'd thought she saw a little of Rob in his easy going charm. Now she was thankful he didn't have the MacLeod propensity for alcoholism on top of her father's. He was far more outgoing and affectionate than any of the Leinos whom she had known her whole life. On the other hand, she knew far less about Ken Miller.

She'd struggled through the holidays. Two days after he left, Rob texted *"Put money in your account for Bobby's Christmas."*

She responded, *"Fuck you,"* but on second thought bought an expensive Apple tablet along with a collection of books and badly needed clothes for Bobby. She knew Rob hadn't told his father about Bobby's paternity, or lack thereof, when an equally expensive mountain bicycle arrived. She didn't interfere when Bobby excitedly called Rob. "Mom, Dad wants to talk to you."

"Tell him I'm busy. I'll call him later." Of course, she wouldn't. "And call your grandfather too." She should start cutting Bobby's ties with the MacLeods but just didn't have the strength to destroy his happiness.

Her stomach churned at her parents' house on Christmas Day as Bobby proudly showed off his tablet and told his cousins about the bicycle. Her son seemed suddenly self-assured, as if he finally discovered the well of his own self-importance. For once he wasn't just the quiet, tagalong, youngest cousin behind Jennie's three older boys and Don's two bored teenagers. She went to the bathroom and vomited.

Jennie was standing outside the door when she opened it. "You sick? You couldn't be pregnant again, could you?"

"Not unless it's a miracle and the father is the Holy Spirit. I don't appreciate you even thinking anything like that."

"What's wrong with you? You either look like somebody just died or you're really prickly."

"It's just the winter. It's just the U.P. I have to get out of here, leave the U.P."

"If there is anything I can do....?"

"There's nothing you can do, maybe I'm just getting sick."

She pleaded illness on New Year's Eve but, sensing Bobby's disappointment, brought him to dinner at her parents' house the following afternoon. Don's absence made the day more bearable. At least, she didn't have to listen to his plans for her in Houston. The thought that circumstances might drive her to Houston just to provide for Bobby, ate at her soul. Her mother commented she seemed to be losing weight and should see a doctor. At least her mother didn't think she was pregnant.

January was long and cold giving her an excuse to stay home. Two large envelopes addressed to Bobby arrived from private schools in Florida. He seemed confused as his grandfather kept telling him about the joys of private college prep and the warmth of Florida winters. At least Rob had kept his vow of silence so far, but she could still imagine her son's prep school days ending with a message his tuition had not been paid because he was an impostor. If he wasn't a MacLeod, who was he? A great inertia overwhelmed her. She was being pulled in too many directions but couldn't move in any of them. Maybe she just didn't want to know who Bobby's father really was. But she had to know, to prepare. She had to find them but couldn't do it while the world was so grey and cold.

♦♦♦

The sun was shining brightly as Meagan got into her car. Finally February. Enough of the Lake was frozen to cut off the supply of humidity that fed the heavy snows. She reached for her sunglasses to blunt the glare of snow reflected sunlight. Bright light and the sudden text had shaken her January lethargy.

"Where are you?" Jennie asked. "You sound like you are in your car."

"Driving into Marquette. Want to pick up some underwear and things for Bobby. Then the MacLeod's lawyer wants to see me about some detail from Rob's last adventures. Something about Paulette Paquette's case, I guess. Might have a nice quiet lunch by myself before I head home."

"Should have told me. I might have come with you."

"Just sort of spur of the moment. Lawyer called late yesterday afternoon, so I thought I might as well get a little shopping done." She made a mental note to swing by Walmart in Marquette to pick up some underwear. You never knew when Jennie might say something to Bobby, even about new undergarments. She had to keep the story straight.

"Nice luncheon yesterday," Jennie continued. "Those Lutheran ladies put on a nice funeral spread. Too bad about old Mary Leino. Did you talk to Todd? Get any gossip on why his wife left him other than that she might have wanted to have a conversation?"

"Just a few words of sympathy and why do you think he'd tell me anything?"

"You did go steady with him for a couple of winters."

"You know how that is. Come fall, only so many boys and so many girls. You have to find someone to cocoon with pretty quick or you'll spend the long winter alone. Only so many choices, doesn't make playing the field a choice. That's why I always liked summer when we had so many options."

"You had options but I didn't. The smart couples broke up for the summers. Jim and I just stayed together. Don't know if it was love or stupidity. I never could understand why you kept going back to Todd every fall. You could have done better."

"It was just easy. He'd been following me around since first grade, so he was always handy. He didn't talk much then either. None of the Leinos did. Wonder what life was like on that God-forsaken farm of theirs."

"Peaceful. If you don't talk, you can't argue, I guess."

"My battery is running low," Meagan wanted to end the conversation. "Have to go. I'll call you later." She stepped on the gas and glanced at the clock. Not a bad idea to go through Marquette anyway rather than take the back roads, especially at this time of the year. The underwear ought to only take a minute at this hour of the morning. Still, almost nine o'clock.

She slowed as she approached the old motel, a low white building with red trim just outside of Ishpeming and pulled around behind the building toward the only unit hidden from the road. She didn't recognize the car but knew it had to be him. She parked, walked to the door, and knocked.

She barely had her arms out of her coat sleeves when Todd pushed her up against the wall and reached under her sweatshirt. He didn't have to struggle with her bra, the one piece of female paraphernalia he'd never been able to conquer, because she had stashed it in her purse before leaving the house. His tongue slide down the side of her neck as his big hands and long fingers messaged her chest. "Magical fingers," the basketball coach had called them for the way they could grasp a ball. Every time she heard that phrase, she smiled.

She shared his frantic impatience. Those long probing fingers pushed aside her jeans as she struggled to step out of them. When she was breathing heavily, he removed his pants and sat on the side of the bed. She straddled him, as his long hands directed her hips in long swaying motions. She stifled a scream and clung to him.

Meagan's relationship with Todd Leino began in the first grade. He was a lonely, awkward boy from a farm south of Thunder Bay his Finnish grandparents had settled a hundred years ago. It was one of those stretches along a secondary road when the forest suddenly gave way to dairy cows feeding in green pastures and hay turning brown in square fields. Not very profitable, most people would say, only for those who did not have the sense to move on. It was a hard and lonely life, especially in an emotionally challenged family.

Todd's parents were tall, thin, and blond as were their sons. Quiet people, they went about their business bereft of conversation. Perhaps being the eldest and emulating his parents, Todd was the most socially awkward of the children. The youngest sibling, Niles, was actually known to laugh and carry on a conversation with strangers, but he was the outlier among the Leinos. At first, the sad looking boy frightened Meagan but she quickly began to think of him as an endearing puppy trying to follow her home.

"Why are you always following me?" she asked him one spring day as they left the schoolyard.

"Because you are pretty and I want to marry you someday," came the answer that at once delighted and horrified her. She liked being admired but had no intention of ever marrying anyone like Todd Leino. She sometimes tried to ignore him during grade school but he just never went away.

They lay naked without touching. His text, *"Motel tomorrow morning,"* had shaken her out of her lethargy. Now she had to find out if he was Bobby's father. He well could be. They'd had sex within a week of Rob coming to her door. She wondered if she should directly suggest paternity to but decided against it. Talking to Todd wasn't easy, his reactions were sometimes unpredictable. He didn't like unplanned things and had a hard time with unexpected developments. Her long history with Todd told her not to suddenly suggest he had an illegitimate son.

She also knew Todd wouldn't talk unless she initiated a conversation and wouldn't touch her again until passion stirred him. Instead they would be still, resting and basking in the afterglow of sex that came close to perfection. Nor did she think it strange that they hadn't spoken. She understood touch was his way of communicating. She broke the silence. "How long are we going to keep doing this, Todd?"

"As long as we want."

"Better yet, why are we still doing this?"

"Because it's nice."

"What about your wife?"

"She has nothing to do with this."

"I hear you are getting a divorce."

"No."

"Separated?"

"Maybe. Why are you asking so many questions? We're not getting divorced. I won't let it happen. That would be wrong. It's not the right order of things."

Todd frequently used that phrase, "the right order of things." Meagan wondered who ordered things in his mind. "Do you love your wife?"

"Why would you ask me that? I guess I do. I don't want her to leave and take the children with her. She's my wife. She should stay. That's the way it's supposed to be."

"And what about me? Do you feel anything for me?"

She didn't know why she asked. She took a psychology class during her one year at Northern Michigan and recognized Todd immediately in the autism spectrum: high functioning, high intelligence Asperger's Syndrome. He was socially awkward, unaware of other people's feelings, and completely focused on problems that interested him. She knew because she'd seen two of his three passions develop. Only his passion for genetic engineering of seeds for frigid climates had eluded her.

When they were freshmen in high school, the basketball coach spotted Todd's height. But he was clumsy and never quite certain of what to do with the ball. He found the school gym perplexing. Why couldn't he get the ball through the hoop as others did? He knew that it was a matter of height, distance, arc, angles, and timing. He studied it and mulled the problem over in his relentless mind. He put a crude basketball hoop in a field and began working out the parameters of the problem. When winter came he moved it into the cattle barn and practiced endlessly amid the warm breath of the dairy herd and the strong scent of manure. He even hooked up a light by the basket so he could practice after dark. By the beginning of their sophomore year, he dazzled the coach with his ability to hit the hoop from almost any angle. He was still clumsy on his feet but his height and ability to score negated much of that.

"Why are you suddenly asking questions? I've always wanted to be with you this way. It is the right order of things. We fit together well."

"We should. You trained me."

"I didn't know any more than you did when we started. I had to find out for both of us. You should be grateful to me."

"I guess I am or I wouldn't be here now."

Todd asked her to go steady at the beginning of their freshman year, the winter before Rob MacLeod started coming into the Ice Cream Shoppe with a whole new way of life and fun. She declined, saying she was too young to go steady. As usual Todd persisted until she agreed a year later. It hadn't turned out badly. With his newly found prowess on the basketball court and outgoing girlfriend, others accepted his peculiarities. Since Todd didn't care about most things, he did what Meagan told him in the sense of what parties they would go to and what movies they would see. He would sit quietly while she talked, even flirted, with other boys and waited for summer to return. And not even her brother Don saw Todd Leino as any threat to her virtue.

Todd didn't touch her until spring began to unfold. He turned down a muddy road and into an old logging trail still banked with snow. "What are we doing here?" she asked.

"I've been thinking. A man should know how to please a woman sexually. I've been reading about it." Most boys would have turned to pornography but Todd had a preference for online medical journals. "I would like to start by touching your tits and observing how you react. Would you mind taking off your blouse and bra?"

She stared at him in disbelief. "Well, if you want to know how to approach women, maybe you should start by learning how to take off their shirts and bras yourself because I don't think a request like that is going to get you very far."

"Oh," he said and reached for the buttons on her blouse.

"Don't you think you ought to try kissing me first? I think that's customary."

"That seems unnecessary for the ultimate act and a good way to spread germs." In all the years she'd known him, he'd never kissed her on the mouth. She thought it odd because later in his pursuit of learning to please a woman, he didn't hesitate to use his mouth and tongue on other parts of her body.

She was certain Todd would have no success at all with women. But he persisted. Finally, she got tired of his fumbling with her buttons and took off her shirt. "Well, you can feel a little but that's all." He struggled with the bra until she finally helped him with that too.

He reached into the back of the truck for a pillow and placed it under her head so she could lean back against the door. "Very nice," he said. "Much prettier than cow tits."

"That's nice to know," she replied as one of his large hands grabbed her breast and pulled. "Todd, that hurts. You're not milking a cow, you know. I think you have to be gentler." His long fingers started at the base of one breasts and pulled gently. "That's better," she sighed. "Much better." His thumbs gently pressed against her nipples. In fact, his variations of motion and pressure became downright pleasant. She closed her eyes and let him continue for a while.

"How long are you going to keep doing this?"

"Until I get it right." Within minutes he gasped, "'oh fuck."

She opened her eyes and followed his to widening stain on the crotch of his jeans. "I hope my mother doesn't notice when she does the wash."

She smiled. "Keep your jacket over it and spill a soda on it when you suit up for the game."

"I'll have to work on this," he said. Thereafter he collected old towels and rags to carefully fold into his pants before further exploring Meagan's body.

Feeling pleasantly warm and relaxed for the first time since Rob's words, Meagan dozed until she felt Todd's hand sliding down the side of her body. Lacking the urgency of their first contact since his visit last summer, Todd worked methodically. He not only incited her obvious erogenous zones but remember she liked him to lightly touch the upper parts of her arms and the area behind her knees. He moved slowly, deliberately until she was moaning.

Again, silence. Again, physical parting. Again, she spoke first.

"Do you have pictures of your children?"

"On my phone."

"Can I see them?"

"Why would you want to do that?"

"I'm just curious."

He sat up and handed her his phone. Meagan examined the family photos. His wife was also tall and blond, her clothing rather ill fitting. If she remembered correctly Todd had met her in a chemistry lab in Ann Arbor, somewhere nobody in Thunder Bay ever expected Todd or any of the other Leinos to be. If it hadn't been for Mr. Symington, his high school chemistry teacher, Todd would still be haunting the dairy barns and hay fields south of Thunder Bay. Todd always got As but never entered into class discussions, so Mr. Symington was startled one day when Todd began talking enthusiastically about his experiments with seed propagation. Todd even referred to serious journal articles he's read online. Mr. Symington helped Todd enter a state science competition. He won first place for his experiments with the genetic properties of cold weather seeds. That led to a scholarship, a wife who worked while he acquired a Ph.D., and rapid advancement in the research division of Monsanto in St. Louis. Everyone in Thunder Bay was stunned.

The two boys looked like Todd. They were tall, blond, and expressionless. His family portraits were singular for their lack of smiles. Meagan wondered why his wife had taken so long to leave him. Maybe she enjoyed the sex as much as Meagan did but Meagan didn't have to earn it by living with him. "Do you spend a lot of time with your children?"

"They're children."

"What does that mean?"

"It's their mother's job to take care of them. That's the right order of things."

No wonder nobody is smiling, Meagan thought. "Do you play games with them and go places with them?"

"I am busy at work. We have a lot of important projects going on right now."

"Do you want to have more children?"

"No. My wife does. She wants a girl."

"And you don't?"

"College tuition is very expensive, so I think two is enough. Besides, I'd have to get the vasectomy reversed."

"Do you have someone like me in St. Louis?"

"Why are you asking?"

"Do you?" She'd learned long ago she had to be demanding to get an answer out of Todd.

"Not now. Once. A woman I worked with. Her husband got suspicious and she quit. I think they moved away."

"Is that why your wife left you?"

"No, she didn't know about it. Just like us. No one did."

"What if this woman got pregnant? What if you had another child by her?"

"You know that wouldn't have happened."

Within a week Todd mastered her breasts, and moved to her genitals. At first she didn't want to take off her jeans but those long, probing fingers left her craving more and deeper contact.

Soon she'd completely disrobe as they drove down shadowed fire lanes and settle back against the pillow and, in winter, covered up with an old blanket he kept in the car. It was sometimes awkward and confining but she let him explore her body at will, shaking and quivering as he tested one spot after another. Years later, on her first visit to a gynecologist, she immediately recognized the first position Todd had forced her into, without of course, the stirrups. Her doctor wondered why she started laughing.

Then one day when spring was almost upon them, he pushed up against her, pressing again and again until she felt the wet stain on his jeans. "I think I'm ready," he said. "Next time I'll bring condoms."

He did. He began as usual, working her into a state of youthful lust before revealing his hard penis. The size shocked her. He unwrapped a condom and put in on, careful that it fit correctly before looking back at her. She was at once fascinated and horrified. "Is it all right? Can I put it in you?" he asked.

"Yes," she answered. "Oh yes."

The careful placement of the condom became part of their ritual until the vasectomy after his second child was born. He told Meagan his wife didn't like all the fuss with the condom but he missed it. Meagan wondered if he considered it a part of "the right order of things."

"That's a silly question," he sounded slightly annoyed. "What would I do if I got someone other than my wife pregnant? I guess I would have to pay her something for an abortion or, if she insisted upon having the child, some kind of payments. I wouldn't want my wife or children to know."

She didn't ask if Todd would want to see such a child, because he didn't seem to want to see his legitimate children. She glanced at her phone. No calls. She reached for her clothes.

"Are you leaving already?"

"It's almost one o'clock. I'm getting hungry."

"Do you want to go somewhere for lunch? Then we can come back."

"We've kept this a secret for so long because we're never seen any place together. Even this motel is taking a chance. Too bad we couldn't get to your trailer, it's a lot safer there." His hand ran up the inside of her thigh. "You're really amazing. I've never seen so much sexual stamina. When you were eighteen maybe, but you never seem to change. Do you take something?"

"No. It's been a long time. My wife doesn't react like you. She did when we were first married but the longer we were married the more she held back. She doesn't take much pleasure in it anymore. It's not the same. I don't know why. I do the same things."

Meagan knew. Being married to someone who can express lust but not love would be a shock to anyone who had not known Todd and his family for a lifetime. His poor wife had to bear emotional scars from being ignored and avoided outside of the bedroom. But Meagan had no way of explaining it to Todd.

"One of the reasons I look forward to coming home" he continued, "and the reason I bought that trailer is to be with you. This…you…are part of coming home …something I look forward to like the Lake and the trees, even the dairy barn. I think of you when I'm with my wife. I thought about you when I was with the other woman. I think of you a lot. And when I go back to St. Louis, I'm going back to an empty motel room."

Meagan knew his few words formed a rare, emotional speech, almost a declaration of love if one substituted love for lust. She had once felt sorry for the excluded, lonely little first grader and now she felt sorry for the emotionally stunted man who still seemed to be following her around. And she was grateful for the dependably best sexual experiences of her life with the only man she knew would never talk about them. She rolled over and ran her hand down his stomach. "I have to leave in one hour," she said. "Next time, bring food."

♦♦♦

She checked the clock as she started her car. She would have enough time to take a shower before Bobby came home. She didn't know when she'd see Todd again, especially since his mother was dead. As she left the motel room, he'd asked if she'd ever consider moving to St. Louis. "Sure Todd," she couldn't help the sarcasm he probably didn't understand. "That way you stop by for a quick fuck before you go home to your wife. No way I'm going to live that way." She ignored the thought that she already was. "You made that decision when you came home at Thanksgiving to tell me…after you screwed me for two days…. you were going to marry another woman."

It wasn't that Meagan wanted to marry Todd. Maybe she clung to Rob and his summer way of life as an alternative to what generally happened to young Yoopers. Unless they left for college or the army, there wasn't much to do but marry your high school sweetheart. At the time she saw that fate as perpetual exile to an isolated, spooky farm filled with a strange race of very mute and very white people. Why marry him when she could summon him for all the sex she wanted without the burden of having to spend the rest of her life with him.

What had really hurt was his explanation. When she asked him why he was going to marry this other woman, he replied, "She's not like you. She won't have sex with me until I marry her. I want to have sex with her so I have to marry her." For the first time in their relationship she'd felt used, like Rob later making her and Bobby pawns in his battles with her father. Even though she realized she'd used Todd as much as he'd used her, she couldn't help thinking of Don's admonitions that boys didn't marry girls who gave themselves too easily.

On the drive back to the MacLeod place, Meagan strained to remember whether Todd had been compulsive about the condom during that fateful Thanksgiving. He must have been. If not, it would have been so out of character she would have remembered. Still, condoms could and did fail.

After Todd told her about getting married, Meagan said she never wanted to see him again. Of course, she had. He came to the MacLeod house when Bobby was about six months old. She told him that she was about to nurse the baby and asked him to leave. He wanted to watch. She told him she would be covered with a blanket but he persisted. He sat there as silently as ever, watching the baby suckle at her breast. Then he put his hand on her jean-covered knee and slid it up her thigh. "Stop that," she demanded.

He didn't move his hand. "I always knew you were having sex with MacLeod too."

She didn't bother to tell him she hadn't until a few days after he announced his engagement. She was tired. She was also getting sexually aroused. She closed her eyes until Bobby finished feeding. Then, with Todd massaging her bare feet and running his hand under her jeans to the hollow behind her knee, Bobby burped. She put the baby into his crib and covered him with a blanket. Todd followed her into her bedroom where they undressed and got into bed. She felt guilty for the first time, not because she'd had sex with Todd, but because she did so with her baby in the next room.

They never really talked about it. They just kept doing it. Whenever Todd was in the U.P., typically two or three times a year, she received a cryptic message indicating where and when. His marriage to the woman who wouldn't have sex with him otherwise, made no difference. When Todd brought his wife home during the first years of their marriage, Meagan wondered how he explained his daylong absences. She never asked. Slowly but surely, Todd's wife stopped visiting the U.P. Meagan wondered if she somehow knew.

After a few initial meetings at the MacLeod estate, Meagan worried that some unexpected visitor would discover them. Todd found several motels on little used roads far enough away from Thunder Bay to provide a sense of security. When Bobby was younger, she had to find a reason for a babysitter and watch the clock carefully. As soon as Todd started at Monsanto, he bought a piece of land on a point jutting out into the Lake not far from the MacLeod estate. He situated an old trailer, not to take advantage of the view, but to be shielded by a clump of pines. Even visitors coming down the driveway would have a hard time detecting it. Once Bobby was in school, especially if the road to Todd's property was snow free, it became easy. Meagan never heard anyone mention Todd's trailer, only that nice piece of property he'd bought for a retirement home someday.

As she headed north, the skies over the Lake filled with gray clouds. More snow. She smiled at the thought her affair with Todd had been their secret for fifteen years. No one knew, even when they were teenagers. Again, Todd formulated a plan. Instead of having sex at the end of the evenings as most of their friends did, Todd picked her up early and drove immediately to one of the many fire lanes and old logging roads crisscrossing the area. He conducted what he called "his experiments," first in elaborate foreplay and later in seeing how many positions a couple could experience in the front seat of a truck, prior to meeting their peers for a dance, party, or movie.

Others only noticed they never touched, much less fell all over each other in teenage fashion, and went directly to their respective houses immediately after every event. Their parents seldom paid much attention when they left their houses, only when they came home at night. No one, even her brother Don, ever suspected their passionate sex life fueled not only by Todd's large appendages but his razor-like mind that treated her body with the same respect with which he approached a basketball. She wondered where her body rated with the genetic makeup of a germinating seed.

She was shocked by her first sexual experience with someone other than Todd. She was seventeen and at a party at Rob's with her crush of the month, Jerry Shane of Grosse Pointe Farms. They'd held hands and wandered down the swimming beach until they were in the shadow of the trees. They sat, kissed, and he put his hand casually in her blouse. They drank some beer and shared a joint. Before she knew it, she was on her back with Jerry barely stimulating her and not properly removing her shorts before pushing his penis toward her. She bolted upright. "What the fuck do you think you're doing? I didn't tell you that you could do that. It's not time to do that and where is your condom? What's wrong with you? Don't you know how to do this right?" Jerry never walked anywhere with her again.

What did she care? Todd didn't object when she told him each May they were breaking up until after Labor Day because she'd be too tired to see him. Between jobs and parties she was too exhausted to dawdle in the front seat of Todd's truck. And if she missed sex, she could always call Todd with "hey, if you have a little time this afternoon, I'd love to catch up on what you've been doing." He always picked her up within half an hour.

Having a secret life of sex, she acquired a reputation for being more of a tease than a dependable sex partner at an evening's end. She didn't mind. At least she got a few hours sleep before getting up for whatever job she had that summer. She confused the summer people by engaging in flirtations and then backing away. And during the winters when the other local girls talked about their sexual adventures, she'd just say, "Well, you know how Todd is." Obviously they didn't.

"Mom," Bobby was home. "Why are you still in your bathrobe. Didn't you get dressed today?"

"Sure. Went to Walmart and bought you some new underwear. It's in your room. I just felt a little dirty when I got home, so I took a shower. Had some of that nasty salt and cinders from the parking lot on me"

She stoked the fire in the little sitting room and fixed hamburgers and a salad with ice cream for dessert. Her trip to

Ishpeming had temporarily removed some tensions from her body but resolved nothing. If Todd was Bobby's father, she didn't want to know because, she realized, she wasn't looking for his biological father as much as a suitable father. Todd might be the best sex partner she ever experienced, but he'd hardly talk to Bobby much less spend hours helping him construct a starship out of Legos. Todd's eyes would never fill with tears in sympathy for a nine-year-old boy. Todd's emotional coldness would destroy Bobby by making him wonder why his father didn't like him. If Todd was Bobby's biological father, she didn't want Bobby to know. Maybe Rob MacLeod was only the second worst father in the world. Poor Todd. He couldn't help the way he was.

♦ ♦ ♦

She received a text at the beginning of March. *"At the farm. Road open. Tomorrow morning."*

She drank coffee until ten before wondering if she should even bother getting dressed or just wear a long coat over her nightgown. But she showered and pulled on some jeans and a sweatshirt, just in case she died en route.

"Where have you been?" Todd's voice startled her.

Since he wasn't pushing her toward the bed, she took a cup and poured some coffee. "What is it, Todd? You're upset about something."

"You're late. I've been here since nine o'clock. It's almost eleven o'clock."

"Sorry. I forgot about your acute sense of order and timing. I hope I'm not wrecking your schedule. Do you want me to leave?"

"No."

"That's right. We haven't screwed yet, have we?" He just stared at her. She knew something was very wrong. She'd learned long ago that Todd largely lived in his own world, oblivious to what those around him were really thinking and doing. He didn't care as long as what was out there didn't impinge on his sense of "the right order of things." Most people saw him as a bit weird but fully functional as he doggedly pursued whatever interested him at the time. But now he had the look of panic she'd only seen once or twice when he realized the discrepancy between his inner life and the outside world. He couldn't understand why. "All right," she said softly. "Tell me what happened. You can tell me. I never tell anyone else."

"She filed for divorce. My wife wants to divorce me. That's not right, but my lawyer says I can't stop her."

"Have you tried? Did you try counseling?"

"Yes."

"And?"

"The counselor said I have problems. I didn't like him."

"Can you change?"

"Nobody can really change."

"That's the most intelligent thing I've ever heard you say."

"I say a lot of intelligent things. The rest of the world is stupid. Sometimes you're stupid but you're always nice to me." She ignored his evaluation of her intelligence because she had sensed years ago their physical contact was one of his few links to the outside world.

She took his hand. "I'd fix it for you if I could, but I can't. Only you and your wife can fix it."

His large hand closed tightly around hers. "I shouldn't have married her. Before she came along, I thought I'd marry you. I should have. She should have let me have sex with her until I could marry you."

Meagan nearly choked on her coffee. "You never asked me to marry you and I don't think it would have worked out anyway. Still, we'll always have each other in our way."

"That MacLeod got in the way. I shouldn't have let you go during the summers."

"Rob MacLeod had nothing to do with you and me. I let you do what you wanted to do, and you let me do what I wanted to do. It was our trade-off."

"If she divorces me, I'll need to marry you. I've thought about it. You can even bring MacLeod's boy to St. Louis with you."

Meagan struggled not to laugh at what was possibly the worst marriage proposal in the history of the world. Did he really think Bobby was an option for her? "Todd, you're upset. Don't say anything you might regret later." She kicked off her shoes and pulled the sweatshirt over her head before reclining on the bed. "Come over here. It will make you feel better."

As his mouth closed in on her breast, she soothed the top of his head. She could feel the tension and unhappiness in him. Marrying Todd was the last thing she ever wanted to do. Still, she wavered; Todd was a path forward, a way out of her present situation. Todd had enough income to provide Bobby with a good education and would undoubtedly spend most of his waking time in his lab. She and Bobby would be alone together; free to do whatever they wished.

She couldn't expect any more from Todd. Since he lived largely in his own head, he certainly couldn't give her anything more than sex and money. Managing him, like now, was sometimes tiresome, but she'd be alone with Bobby most of the time. She could do whatever she wanted; free to pursue an education, her own career, or make new friend without him. Still, Todd's influence on Bobby would be negative, perhaps devastating. She remembered Rob's reflections on feeling unloved by his father. She just couldn't do that to Bobby.

Nor could she do it to herself. She instinctively knew once she made her pact with this particular devil, she could never break it. Once she married a flawed man who could never love in an unselfish way, she would never have the heart to set him adrift in a world he didn't fully understand. She felt sorry for his wife who probably had no idea what she was getting into when she married him and was probably confused by him now. She just couldn't do it. She once again mentally and finally negated Todd from Bobby's life. She now had to take the next step and look for the other possible father, Ken Miller.

CHAPTER 6

As he sat down at his laptop, Ken Miller pulled a blanket around his shoulders in a search for warmth. The glare of late February sunlight bouncing off the ice clad Lake flooded the small kitchen of his tiny rental. Fucking Lake. Fucking cold. He wondered how he'd gotten from Oklahoma to this God-forsaken tundra with its endless winters. At least it wasn't overcast. At least he wasn't in Marquette, Michigan with well over a hundred inches of snow every year. Duluth, Minnesota, built on a hill at the western end of the 350-mile long Lake, only had a modest 85-inch average annual snowfall. He remembered his disbelief when, upon his arrival in Marquette, someone told him to equip his car with a red flag hoisted on a tall pole so other drivers would know he was approaching intersections. He couldn't fathom the idea until he found himself driving through canyons of snow.

He scrolled through his email, clicking off annoying advertisements, offers, and cute little sayings from former students. Meagan. Meagan who, he wondered. He hesitated but clicked. *"Hi Ken, Remember me? Northern Michigan ten years ago. Just playing an old Yooper winter game of 'what ever happened to' and came across your mailbox. Hope your life has gone well. Meagan Flannigan."* He held his hand over the delete button but hesitated and went on. Nothing good had come from his life in the Upper Peninsula. Compared to Marquette, Duluth was almost civilized.

Fifteen minutes and another cup of coffee later, he remembered. Yes, Meagan Flannigan had been a bright spot in his two years as an instructor at Northern Michigan; a bright, pretty girl with an infectious smile, a radiant warmth, and a great body. She'd been in his freshman history class and, in spite of university rules against such things, he found her very attractive. Still, he hadn't acted until mid-semester when she walked into a pub near the campus with her female roommate.

Yes, it was all coming back to him. He had been pressing her to move into his apartment when they'd had a fight over something silly. In fact, he'd thought of marrying her, even asked her, if he recalled correctly. She hadn't said "no," but never seemed too serious about the idea. In spite of a lifetime with his mother, he'd optimistically thought marriage might be a solution to his loneliness. Meagan Flannigan. Sure, she had drifted in and out of his consciousness for years. If Meagan Flannigan had not abruptly disappeared, everything might have been different.

He scrolled back and took a second look at her email. How was his life? Not great but he wasn't going to tell her that.

"Sure I remember you. I'm fine. Whatever happened to you? I looked but you vanished. Did you finish your degree? I completed the dissertation and moved on to a post-doctorate at Indiana for two years. Did a stint at a junior college outside Minneapolis for a while and landed at the University of Minnesota at Duluth. I'm on a tenure track, so might decide to stay. Just divorced. Great to be back in the single life. Where are you?"

He read his note. The stark truth was he'd finally finished the dissertation, hadn't been able to get anything, published, and searched for a secure, tenured position ever since. He didn't want to spend his life in Duluth but nobody gave up a possibly permanent job unless he had a better offer. And one of the ways to get a better offer was to already have tenure someplace else. It made a job candidate look more desirable and provided leverage in negotiations. But if he didn't get something published soon, he wouldn't even get tenure at a God-forsaken place like Duluth.

The alternative was depressing. The once dependable academic world was now a growing quagmire. Like American business, American universities had discovered cheap, part-time labor. Adjunct, meaning part-time professors without benefits, filled teaching schedules making full-time jobs increasingly scarce. He knew too many people going from one part-time teaching job to another with increasingly little chance of ever living above poverty level.

Nor was he about to mention he'd met and married Emily within six months of Meagan's sudden departure. Emily, a graduate student from Belfast, was looking for, among other things, a husband who could ease her entry into the United States. After several hysterical episodes during which she threatened suicide rather than returning to a place she claimed to loath, Ken agreed to marry her. He'd figured it didn't matter because he'd learned from his mother that marriages are eternally negotiable and easily ended. When it was over, it would simply be over; just another episode and a series of episodes called life. While he sometimes fantasized about finding the eternal soul mate who would bring him happiness, he knew in the depths of his soul such a person did not exist. Still, he dreamed and reached out for that elusive perfect union.

Emily was very bright, in economics, and had published an article as a graduate student so was academically desirable. She easily found positions at universities that didn't particularly want Ken. The University of Indiana, where Emily did her Ph.D., arranged a two-year post-doctoral slot for him, but while she went straight to an assistant professorship at the University of Minnesota at Minneapolis, all he could find was a temporary junior college job.

Marriage didn't make him happy either. Several affairs with students led to more of Emily's screaming. Eventually, he began avoiding her. They were barely speaking when she had an offer from the University of Pennsylvania. "You might as well go by yourself," he told her, "because this marriage certainly isn't working. We're both miserable, so let's just end it and get on with our lives." She agreed. No hysterics this time. She had her degree, her citizenship, and a good job. She'd never see working class Belfast again.

Divorce didn't make Ken happy either. He was initially thrilled to find an assistant professorship but once he'd moved into a small, three-room apartment whose kitchen shared Duluth's communal view of Lake Superior, his spirits sank. He missed having another person around, even someone he tried hard to ignore. He regretted the divorce. Loneliness settled over him until he had trouble getting out of bed in the mornings and revising articles necessary for being voted tenure. He stood by the window watching the lift bridge rise to allow an ore ship push through the ice and into the inner harbor.

Warm memories filled his consciousness. He thought Meagan Flannigan was just a flirtatious, amusing girl from some remote village until he got her into bed, a feat that took some time and effort. He'd anticipated being the older man guiding her in the ways of sexuality. But she was not only self-assured but knew exactly what she wanted. Yes, Meagan Flannigan had once made him very happy. Maybe she could make him happy again.

She wouldn't have contacted him, he mused, if she wasn't interested in renewing some kind of relationship. She'd always made him feel good. What the shit had they fought about? He hoped she was within driving distance because his salary didn't cover luxuries like frequent trips to distant cities. He went back to the kitchen table and hit "send."

◆◆◆

Meagan stared at the computer screen, wondering if he would answer her. Her recent days with Todd had energized her enough to start a Goggle search for the other man who could be Bobby's father. At first she despaired. The world was full of Ken Millers. She narrowed the name down to the academic world but was about to give up when she found a Ken Miller in the history department at the University of Minnesota at Duluth. Fortunately his faculty profile included a photo. She stared at it, trying to decide if she had the right person. Well, she concluded, she didn't have much to lose.

The quick reply startled her. He remembered her, or at least said that he did. He seemed mildly interested. Hard to tell. What should she tell him? She couldn't just bluntly ask him to spit in a tube in order to find out if he was the father of her son. Better to go slowly. Initiate a conversation. See if her memories matched reality. Assess what kind of a parent he would be. Maybe he wouldn't even want to know. After all, theirs was only a yearlong relationship that ended a decade ago.

"Hi, Sorry I left so suddenly. Family, personal problems. Had to go home. Derailed me for a couple of years but now I'm

interested in going back to school. I was hoping you were still at NMU to advise me. I live about an hour west of Marquette, managing an estate for a wealthy family. Fun summers but quiet winters. I'm thinking of a degree in history. Can you recommend some reading?"

She smiled. She could hardly write the unvarnished truth; that she had to leave Marquette because she was knocked up and he was now a prime suspect. Nor could she report spending most of the last decade hiding in one of the most isolated places in the country while thinking someone else was the father of her son. If she went back to school, it wouldn't be in history but something with a better economic future. And she couldn't say her life was as dull as dust, only punctuated by visits from her married, autistic lover or her bossy, argumentative brother.

What else, she wondered. She tried to remember if he had any friends and finally retrieved two names and continued. *"Whatever happened to Scott Reagan and Jack Warren? And the dissertation? How did that go? Didn't it have something to do with Native Americans? Interesting subject."* Dumb reply, she thought but pressed send.

Ken Miller's basic U.S. History class hadn't impressed Meagan. He seemed bored as he ran through his notes only modernized by a power point presentation that wasn't much different than chalk on the blackboard, except for requiring much more expensive equipment. For some strange reason she never understood, a computer assigned her to U.S. History Since 1865 in her first semester and U.S. History Before 1865 in the second semester. But, since she'd had American History during her senior year in high school, she already knew that the Revolutionary War came before the Civil War and not visa-versa as it was now being presented to her.

Mr. Miller was younger than most of the faculty but still a decade older than she was. The class was large and Meagan sat in the back. She had no idea he even noticed her until she walked into the Hangout, a saloon with low ceilings and Northern Michigan pennants on the walls. She barely noticed him as she walked past the bar. "Are you enjoying the class, Miss Flannigan?"

He was sitting on a bar stool but she already knew he was of medium height and on the thin, wiry side. Now she noticed his round head, anxious smile and deep blue eyes. "Yes, it is very interesting."

"Are you here alone?"

"I'm with my roommate," she nodded toward Sue, a tall, quiet girl who reminded her a little of Todd.

"Can I buy the two of you a beer, or maybe I should say two beers?"

She couldn't very well say "no," so asked him to join them. He was a more interesting conversationalist than he was a lecturer. After politely asking about their backgrounds, he insinuated he was not only accustomed to living in much larger cities but had traveled extensively. Only later did she discover his travels were courtesy of the United States Army. She recognized academic name-dropping but didn't recognize the names, so just smiled at what she considered the right places. He spoke glibly about writing a doctoral dissertation as if everyone was doing it. He proclaimed his political liberalism, religious atheism, and general goodwill to all humankind. He pointed out his use of "humankind" as a sign of his support of feminism.

He reached such an exuberant high after consuming a second beer that she kiddingly asked him what he had been doing all afternoon. He looked at her strangely and answered, "after I finished my class, I did some research and writing."

"How long have you been here?"

"Just five minutes before you came in. Why?"

She smiled. "Just wondering how professors spend their time." What she wanted to say was that she'd never seen anyone get inebriated so easily on so little alcohol. "Where are you from? Originally." She knew anyone from the U.P. was genetically incapable of getting high on two beers.

"I'm not a professor, just a lowly instructor. Midwest and the Plains. We moved around a lot. My mother works in the oil industry. My father is in sales. They divorced when I was little. "

He reeked of outsider; someone who'd blown in on an academic wind and couldn't wait to move on. Still, the way he zeroed in on her while ignoring her roommate was flattering. When they rose to leave, he insisted upon driving them the few blocks to their apartment. He jumped out of his old car and walked them to their door. Once Sue was inside, he pulled Meagan back and kissed her on the forehead. "See you in class," was all he said.

Strange guy, she thought, as she closed the apartment door behind her. Although she was close to home, Meagan was suddenly among people she hadn't known all of her life. It was a little disconcerting and left her feeling a bit disorientated. He certainly was not just another Yooper boy.

The laptop pinged. *"My dissertation is on the origins of Native American casinos. What kind of history are you interested in reading?"*

She thought the answer a no-brainer. *"I'd forgotten the subject of your dissertation. Must be your influence because I'm fascinated by Native American history. I'd love to read some of the stuff you've written."*

He replied. *"Great. Have to teach a class now but will send you a reading list later. Also an article I'm working on. Maybe you'll have some suggestions."*

Meagan smiled. She had him temporarily hooked. Now all she had to do was probe to see if he was open to being a father and what kind of father he would be.

♦♦♦

Ken Miller overwhelmed her. He bought coffee after class and insisted on driving her wherever she wanted to go. Unlike Todd, he hung on her every world and whim. Unlike Rob, he seemed devoted only to her. He listened to her ideas and encouraged her to do well in all of her classes, even the ones she didn't like. She liked the attention, although his manner bordered on obsequiousness. By the time she went to Thunder Bay for Christmas, she felt she had found an emotional anchor in Marquette.

She'd thought of asking Ken to visit her family on Christmas but decided against it. She didn't think her family, particularly her brother Don, would like or understand his denunciation of Christmas as a myth much less his stand against hunting on the grounds of animal abuse. Conversely, he might not like her family's Yooper sensibilities. And Todd would be home from Ann Arbor. She might be able to handle a lover and a potential boyfriend if Ken only came for a few hours of Christmas dinner, but Ken had developed a habit of hanging around a little too long.

After the Christmas break Ken spent more and more time at her apartment. "Why is he here again?" Sue was clearly annoyed. "This is the third time this week you've fixed dinner for him."

"I didn't know you objected and he bought the groceries. And be quiet, he's in the living room, he can hear you."

"I pay half the rent and he's always here." When Sue was agitated her voice became loud and shrill. "When we agreed to be roommates, I didn't know a boyfriend would be part of the deal."

Meagan suspected the awkward Sue was angry because she resented Meagan's ease with men. The obvious solution was a new roommate but that presented several problems. Since Don was paying the bulk of Meagan's expenses, he expected a detailed accounting. She'd have to explain why she or her roommate had moved. If the truth came out, Don certainly wouldn't approve of a relationship with an older man. Don would probably pressure her to do what he wanted her to do in the first place which was to move into a dorm.

Ken stood smiling in the doorway. "I have an idea. Instead of dinner here, let's go out, do something festive for a change."

Meagan glanced at Sue. "Great idea. Let me get some things together first." She repacked the bag of instant slaw mix, frozen chicken pot pies, baking potatoes, butter and rolls into a paper bag. She wasn't going to leave any of Ken's food for Sue.

They walked out into the darkness of a late January afternoon. "Sorry about that. I moved in with her before I really knew her. She from the Mitten; I met her and her mother in the housing office. There was a problem with my dorm room reservation and she wanted to rent an apartment. I figured I could share one with her, and cook my own food, for the same price as the dorm room."

"Where's Mitten?"

She laughed as they got into Ken's old Toyota. "The Mitten is the Lower Peninsula. Look at it on a map. It looks like a mitten. I keep forgetting that you don't speak the language. I don't know why she is up here. She probably couldn't get in anyplace else. Where are we going?"

"How about the Border Grill or the Rice Paddy. Or we could cook at my place." He was secretly pleased because he'd been looking for ways to get her to spend more time at his place where they would be alone.

"No, you promised me a restaurant meal." She had hoped for something nicer than cheap tacos or inexpensive Thai but had noticed Ken's unwillingness to spend much money on food. At the time she presumed it was the result of the low salary he repeatedly mentioned.

"What about the groceries?"

"You can take them home. Maybe tomorrow night…or the next time you're not busy…at your place."

They both knew they were engaged in a delicate dance. She innocently introduced him as "my friend," as if to say anything other than friendship is not only impossible but also ludicrous. He possessively put an arm around her when they were with his friends as if to say of course I'm having a steamy affair with this beautiful young girl. He had great faith their relationship would progress to his desired level while she hadn't made up her mind as yet.

The longer they were together, the more convinced he became of her innocence. Whenever he leaned his head towards hers, she seemed oblivious to the fact that he wanted to kiss her. When he tried to push his tongue beyond her lips, she was startled. He was certain his newly found attempt-to-find-love had never experienced sexual passion, so he reasoned he had better tread slowly. She, on the other hand, became intoxicated with his desire to please her and the knowledge she could probably get him to do about anything she wanted. She basked at the center of his world.

After tacos and beer, she insisted on going home. After coffee the following day, he told her that he was meeting another instructor for help with his dissertation. Thinking she had no easy way out of living with Sue, Meagan made peace by asking her roommate if she wanted to go to a movie. Once in line at the ticket office, she saw Ken with a rather attractive female several customers ahead of them.

Ken's expression passed from shock, to horror, and then misery when he saw Meagan staring at him. Amusement spread across Meagan's face as she smiled and waved. He looked like the mouse caught in the trap while she looked like the cat waiting to devour him. She and Sue weren't home fifteen minutes when he was at her door.

"Did you get a lot of editing done?" she asked as he walked into their living room and Sue slammed the bedroom door.

"Look, she did help me and then said she wanted to go to that movie. I mean, what else could I do? I couldn't very well say 'no.'"

Fully aware that he was more serious about her than she was about him, she laughed, "But the real question is whether she said 'no'."

Of course he couldn't tell Meagan he felt obligated to take Nancy to the movie because she'd asked just as they'd finished having sex. Now a desperate fear of losing Meagan overwhelmed him. "It wasn't like that," he swore. "She was just helping me with my writing. I don't feel anything for her but you're special. I think I'm in love with you. I'll never see her again."

Meagan kept smiling and wondering if she should put the poor man out of his misery. In retrospect, she should have realized the girl in the movie line was just the first warning.

Meagan played with him until spring began to melt the winter's snow. He became increasingly ardent, insisting he wanted to marry her. Then one night she brought her toothbrush and a change of underwear to his apartment. She let him kiss her without objecting. He pushed her toward the tiny bedroom, "I presume you have condoms. I don't want to get pregnant."

His hands went slack on her shoulders. "Condom? Shit that's old fashioned. Aren't you on birth control of some kind? I thought all girls took care of that these days."

"Well, I haven't. And then there is the question of sexually transmitted diseases."

He'd expected a wildly magic moment, not this coldly pragmatic conversation. "What exactly do you want?"

"Condoms. Or I'm going home."

"All right. All right." His budding erection began to fail. "Whatever you say. Just stay here. I'll be back as soon as I can."

When he finally got back into bed, Ken was shocked. The girl who didn't know how to kiss a man properly and demanded a condom seemed to have a secure knowledge of everything else. Only in the middle of the night did he understand why she had asked for condoms in the plural. The girl was voracious.

◆◆◆

Meagan stared at the laptop. "What are you doing, Mom?"

"Just helping an old friend with some of his work."

"What kind of work?"

"He's a teacher who needs some help with his homework,"

"I didn't know teachers had homework."

"They do."

"Dad says he's going someplace called Belize."

She looked up. "You still skype with your dad a lot, don't you?" She had expected Rob would inevitably get bored with Bobby. As much as she didn't want to see her son hurt, the cessation of their conversations would make it easier to tell Bobby the truth someday...whenever she couldn't avoid it anymore.

"Sometimes we talk on my phone. Sometimes he says he's sick and would rather not have me see him."

"Why is he going to Belize?"

"I don't know. Why don't you ask him?"

"Maybe I will someday. Has your grandpa mentioned anything about your dad?"

"No. He just wants us to move to Florida. Are we?"

"No, not if I can help it. I have to work some things out before we tell your grandfather we're never moving there."

"Uncle Don says we're moving to Texas. Why do people think we're moving?"

"Because people don't know your mom very well. We might move someday. In fact we probably will because I'd like you to go to better schools with more opportunity. But we're only going where we decide to go, where we think is the best of us. Don't pay any attention to your Uncle Don either."

"What does Dad want us to do?"

"He says he wants us to be happy."

She looked down at the laptop. Ken's article was really boring.

♦♦♦

Elation overwhelmed Ken as he read the letter accepting his article on the 1842 Battle of Bois Brule between the Dakota Sioux and Lake Superior Ojibwe. One reader commented on the vast improvement in organization and style. He'd followed Meagan's few structural suggestions and grammatical corrections but assured himself the work was all his. After all, she didn't even have a bachelor's degree. Maybe Meagan was his good luck charm. He reached for his phone to text her. She sent back congratulations

"Hey, how about driving over to Duluth for a little celebration. I can put you up for the night. Best behavior. You can have the bed; I'll take the sofa."

"Love to but I'd need a babysitter."

"Babysitter????"

"I have a son. Haven't I mentioned that?"

"No. When were you married?"

"I wasn't. Single mother and all that."

Ken's antenna went up. *"How old is he, or is it she?"*

"He's nine years old."

Oh shit, Ken thought. Is that what this is all about? Ten years ago they were practically living together in Marquette. He wanted to ask the kid's exact birth date but thought it too crude. And if she was trying to blame this kid on him, why hadn't she done so nine years ago? Maybe she was having money problems. Ken started to ask if she knew who the father was but thought the outright question too rude. *"Can I ask about the lucky guy?"*

She could almost read the panic in his words. Not a good sign. *"The birth certificate and a DNA test both say Robert James MacLeod is the father. His parents own the estate I manage. I'd known Rob for years before Bobby was born. Do you have any children?"*

"Not to my knowledge."

"Do you want children?"

He was going to make that clear right now. *"No. Was an only child and quite frankly I don't think it is fair to bring a child into this world with global warming, population pressures, etc. It might come off as selfish but, no, I've never wanted to have children and don't intend to. Don't think I'd make a good father anyway."*

"If you don't think so, you probably wouldn't. But no, I can't drive to Duluth because I have a nine year old son."

"Too bad. I think we would have had fun. Anyway, thanks a lot for your help. I appreciate it." Something told him to add something like 'so good-by forever. Don't call me; I'll call you.' He stared out at the Lake. It would have been so nice. He had such great memories of her and thought she'd be a real asset to his career. As the icy winter Lake stretched out before him, he felt himself slipping into depression.

He had a second thought. Children didn't always make much difference. After his parents' divorce, he'd moved, sometimes in the middle of the night, from one small town to another with his mother who was always broke and always looking for a man to take care of her. Once when economically desperate, she left him with her parents in Bartlesville, Oklahoma. While his grandparents' white frame house seemed almost palatial compared to their series of cheap apartments, it was also emotionally cold and lonely. His mother's promise of "a couple of weeks", turned into almost two years. As he recalled, Meagan had a big family capable of taking care of her *son. Sure he's a great kid. Just wanted to let you know how I feel up front. I hope we can still be friends. I'd still like to see you sometime....with or without the kid.*

I have a corner with a sleeping bag for him." He really didn't mean the latter. Kids scared him. He wouldn't really know what to do with a kid. His own childhood had been so miserable that he didn't want to inflict his experiences on anyone.

"Sure. Fine. Have to go. Have a painter down in the boathouse. Turning it into a summer rental." Ken Miller was turning out to be a real bummer. Instead of joining Jim in the boathouse, Meagan sat staring out at the Lake. Sunlight caught an icicle at the corner of the roof, causing it to drip into the snowdrift below. Meagan knew it was still too early; that the first signs of fluidity would only freeze again tonight. Ken Miller. What, in her youthful hubris, had she seen in him? Devotion. A much greater need to be loved than she had ever experienced. She suddenly realized she had never felt completely unloved. Except maybe for that week or two in Marquette resulting in Bobby.

♦ ♦ ♦

Ken deluged Meagan with short texts reminding her of things they had done together. She didn't fully understand why he wanted to keep in contact with her, but he obviously did. She already knew what she wanted to know; namely that Ken Miller had no interest in being a father to anyone and would undoubtedly balk at taking any kind of test. He seemed to have no knowledge of fatherhood. Ken only gave her vague answers about his own father. The man had run off with a woman from work and moved to Kansas City where he became a beer salesman. The stepmother, who gave birth to three half siblings, didn't hide her resentment of Ken's existence. Consequently, Ken had rarely seen his father and had very little communication with him. Of Ken's many stepfathers, he only remembered one with any degree of fondness.

He summed up his numerous references to their long talks, quiet times, and shared meals with *"that little apartment was the closest thing I had to a home for a long time before and after."* Wow, Meagan thought. She remembered his little apartment as cramped, crowded, and messy. She thought of cleaning it but didn't want to fall into her mother's pattern of following her father around and picking up after him. So she'd waited until he started cleaning and helped. She recalled cooking only on the condition that he did the dishes. It might be nice and cozy on a winter night but she'd hardly considered it homey.

The daily texts revived distant memories of their conversations. He liked playing the older intellectual often expounding on his beliefs, thoughts, and experiences. He described his grandparents taking him to their Southern Baptist Church, where their hell, fire, and brimstone preacher gave him nightmares. He'd learned early to provide for himself. Starting at the age of 12, he always had after-school jobs as neither his mother nor his stepfathers ever gave him any spending money. He cobbled together a series of jobs, grants, and loans to get through college; hanging around the history department flattering his professors until they wrote recommendations for a graduate assistantship. He devoted his summers to whatever paid best, from janitorial to construction to factory work. Still, he sometimes slept on friend's sofas, showered at the gym, studied in the library, and lived on ramen noodles.

Meagan looked at Bobby and wondered how he would feel about being left with her parents or having to earn his own spending money. She felt sorry for Ken but admired his pluck. A largely unwanted kid from the hardscrabble hills of northeastern Oklahoma had invented himself as an academic. Not everyone possessed the brains, ambition, and grit to do so.

He looked up his old Marquette friends so he could report their doings to Meagan. *"Hey, didn't you have a roommate? A strange girl who never said much. Whatever happened to her?"*

Meagan stared at her phone. He remembered lectures and musical programs they had attended but didn't remember what happened with Sue? She recalled very graphically. Thanksgivings bookmarked their relationship. She met Ken around Thanksgiving of her freshman year. When she went home for Thanksgiving her sophomore year, Todd told her that he was going to marry the girl who wouldn't have sex with him but would work to put him through school. Distraught at Todd's unexpected announcement she decided to catch a ride back to Marquette on Saturday evening rather than waiting for Sunday afternoon. When she entered her apartment, she heard soft music, saw empty beer bottles in the living room, and listened an unmistakable squeaking bed.

"As I recall I came back early from Thanksgiving with my family and found you in bed with Sue. At least you were using her bed and not mine. I think you pleaded drunkenness which didn't make Sue very happy. She just kept sobbing. I can't recall what I said but it was enough to make the two of you leave. I put all of your, and Sue's, belongings into plastic trash bags and threw them outside. I had the lock changed in the morning and went to class. I never knew if you or the trash man took your stuff but the bags were gone when I got home. Sue didn't come back to the apartment and never contacted me. I presumed you gave Sue shelter, and whatever, for the night or maybe more. It was the last time I saw either one of you. Haven't the slightest idea of whatever happened to Sue. Thought you might have a better idea."

"Fuck. I'd completely forgotten the whole incident. I must have really been drunk. That has to rank as one of the worst, if not the absolute worst, mistake of my life. I was really stupid. I hope that isn't the reason why you left school. Shit, I really feel terrible."

"No, that incident is not why I left school. An old friend from Thunder Bay came by a day or two later and cheered me up for about a week. Then I went home for the weekend and just never went back."

She didn't add that she could no longer pay the rent, so packed everything and returned home. She told her family that she was sick and stayed in bed for two weeks. Then she started throwing up in the mornings.

While the memory of the Sue and Ken incident initially infuriated her again, within minutes she saw it as funny. Ken not only lacked the ability to play a fatherly role but also had no idea as to fidelity of any kind. She wondered briefly why all of the men in her life were so flawed and concluded it was part of the human condition. Although she had pretty well checked Ken Miller off her potential father list, she continued answering his texts, but for no particular reason.

◆◆◆

Meagan mentioned a weekend trip to Hurley on the Wisconsin border. Ken clicked on Google Maps. He'd initially checked the distance between Duluth and Marquette, only 282 miles, but living in a land where the only interstates went due south to Minneapolis or Chicago, 282 miles meant a five and a half hour drive under the best conditions. Once she mentioned living in the old mansion, he'd hinted but she had not invited him to visit. Since he thought paying for motel was a waste of money when you could stay with a friend or sleep in your car, a free room would make the trip more feasible. Then she mentioned the child. Maybe the child made his visit untenable, or perhaps she had a partner after all. He asked a few more questions whose answers negated a partner and hinted again but to no avail.

Hurley put Meagan a little over 100 miles and two hours closer to him. He couldn't just invite himself to her family celebration, so he looked for reasons to be close to Hurley. He could easily be doing research at the two Ojibwe reservations between Duluth and Hurley. Madeline Island, the old trading center of the Lake Superior Ojibwe, was another possibility until he realized that he'd have to pay a substantial car ferry fee to get to and from the Island.

"What a coincidence. I'm planning on doing some research on Ojibwe legends at Red Cliff and Bad River about the same time. Maybe we could meet for lunch or something. Really would love to see you."

He'd been to both places. Red Cliff's casino was on the Lake and more conducive to romance. The Bad River casino sat astride the main highway, trying to net passing tourists just as the Ojibwe once netted fish from fast flowing streams. But Bad River was closer to Hurley and most likely to entice her.

The gray skies made it harder and harder for Ken to work. He knew his sinking feeling usually preceded the bouts of depression. He'd suffered through them alone until finally seeking help in Duluth after what he mistook for a heart attack. Once he and Sue fled Meagan's apartment, he'd spun into a then undiagnosed depressive cycle. He remembered looking at Sue but thinking of Meagan, intuitively knowing he had once again made a horrible mistake. He recalled Sue saying something about going home to that Mitten place and she too disappeared.

By the time the untreated depression began to lift, Ken had another problem. During his down time, students had complained about him not showing up to teach his classes. The Dean let him know, although the university would honor the remainder of his contract rather than challenge his claims of illness, Ken's contract would not be renewed for another year. Still in a state of partial funk, he went to a party where Emily introduced herself by sitting on his lap and asking how she could cheer him up.

"I might be able to get away for a couple of hours. Since it's my aunt and uncle's fiftieth wedding anniversary, all of their children and grandchildren will be in Hurley and the parties will go on for days. I'll ask my sister if she can keep an eye on Bobby for one afternoon."

♦ ♦ ♦

Ken hesitated. The bar/lounge at the Bad River Casino was dark with the sounds of gaming machines in the background. She stood in the doorway, partially blinded by the transition from the sunlight. He decided it had to be her and waved. She sat down at the table where he was sipping coffee. The conversation began awkwardly. "So nice to see you again, Meagan. You haven't changed." She had, of course. He missed a certain youthful freshness about her, a certain openness of smile, and eagerness for life. Maybe they had once been there or maybe he'd just imagined them.

"Nice to see you too. You haven't changed much either. Hair is a little grayer perhaps." He obviously did not like her observation.

He asked about her drive and her family. She told him her sister had readily agreed to take Bobby when she told her she was meeting a man. "My family worries about me," she laughed. "They think I live in isolation."

He saw an opening to probe her romantic situation. "I hope their wish comes true. And the boy's father? You aren't still with him?"

"No, no." She wasn't going to fall into that trap. "That was just one of those things. She changed the subject. "Tell me about you. Your marriage just ended?"

He fell into talking about how he and Emily had seemed so right for each other, how their mutual interests joined, but how their career paths took them in opposite directions. That, of course, was his public slant on his marriage. He didn't remember much about the wedding other than Emily's tears, threats, and demands. In retrospect, he was depressed and didn't care if he married her or not.

"It sounds like a great marriage. Couldn't you have worked something out, like finding jobs in the same area or commuting?"

"I find that if you can't be together on a full time basis, it is just as well to end it and move on. My observation is one needs to be with a soul mate to be happy. I haven't found, or missed, mine."

"That's interesting. I've always thought happiness comes from within. A good marriage involves two people who were already happy with themselves."

"That's what psychiatrists say but I don't believe them."

She took her turn in asking pointed questions. "Did your wife want a family?"

"No. We were of one mind there. She also felt this world is not a proper place to raise children. Besides, there is so much to enjoy without them."

If this world was not the proper place to raise children, she wondered, where was? "I'm sure you must have other prospects by now. You were never in need of female companionship."

"I wish. It's easy to meet women but not the right kind of woman."

"And what kind are you looking for?"

"Someone bright and intelligent, someone who shares my interests. A companion as well as a lover. Say, what about lunch? The restaurant is having a taco special."

"No." Her decisiveness startled him. She wasn't quite the Meagan of his memories. A decade ago she wasn't as quick and firm in her decisions. "It's too nice a day to sit inside like this. The sun is shining and the temperature is above freezing for a change. Let's drive up the road to Ashland and find someplace with windows. Unless you want to gamble, that is."

"I'm not much of a gambler, at least not at places like this. I play the stock market a little but haven't had much success at it. Besides, I'm still up to my neck in student debt."

He chose a café that drew tourists off the highway as well as providing endless coffee for some of the natives. It had a wide view but of traffic on the highway. The hamburgers were mediocre but the conversation picked up when he talked about his research. He explained he grew up among the Osage around Bartlesville and watched the proliferation of Native American casinos throughout Oklahoma. As the state was once the dumping ground for unwanted native peoples from the east, tribe after tribe, from the Cherokee to the Choctaw to the Seminole and even the Comanche, vied for a piece of Oklahoma's "new buffalo economy." His master's thesis was on gaming in Oklahoma and his dissertation on a broad overview of gaming in the trans-Mississippi West. He found courses in the local native history popular in the northern Great Lakes, so was drawn in that direction. Hence, his article on the Battle of Bois Brule.

With the waitress circling their table, Meagan offered to buy beer at a hotel with a nice view of the Lake. The large, white building at the end of Chequamegon Bay was designed to look a lot older than it was. As they settled near the wide windows of the otherwise deserted, old fashioned bar, the conversation drifted back to his work. She made suggestions. Why didn't he concentrate on how the past affected the present in the Upper Great Lakes? For example, how did the early Sioux-Ojibwe-Winnebago patterns of competition and co-operation influence the present day gaming economy and culture? In the recent past the Winnebago (now known as the Ho-Chunk) successfully waged a political war to block the Ojibwe from expanding into southern Wisconsin while the Shakopee Mdewakanton Sioux of Prior Lake, Minnesota had financed the new Ojibwe casino at Red Cliff.

"Exactly, he said," as if he'd originated the idea. "Yes. Definitely." He was impressed by Meagan's thinking. Where might he be today if he hadn't gotten drunk and into bed with Sue? Or married Meagan instead of an economist with absolutely no interest in his work? Once back in Duluth, he'd have to start fleshing out Meagan's ideas.

"Do you ever think of leaving the U.P.?" He didn't want to give her too much intellectual credit.

"Yes, sometime in the future, maybe even the near future."

"Do you have any specific plans?"

"I have options. My brother wants me to move to Houston. I have a friend who wants me to move to St. Louis and my son's grandparents want us to move to Florida."

"So why haven't you done any of the above?"

"Because I don't really want to do any of them."

"I take it your son's grandparents have some money."

"Yes. They want him to go to private schools." She didn't say there could be a possible problem if Bobby ever had another DNA test.

"Then your problem is solved," he advised. "Go with the money."

She smiled. "Money isn't everything. I've known some pretty miserable rich people. I don't want my son to be one of them."

"I'll give you another option. Duluth." He wondered why he was saying this. Perhaps because he'd mentally rehearsed the words before meeting her. "You'd be close to your family and yet far enough away to be free of them. Your son's grandparents can pay for his schooling in Duluth or maybe even a boarding school. I'd do everything possible to help you."

She smiled again and rose. "Thank you for your offer." She had no intention of becoming an academic wanderer with the likes of Ken Miller. Life with him was not what she envisioned for herself much less for her son. "I really have to be getting back. We're invited to a cousin's house tonight."

"Do you really have to go?" he asked. "I could get a room." He wondered how much a room in this place would cost him. At least an afternoon of sex might be fun.

She looked down at him. "I really can't stay. I really just came for lunch and a little conversation...which has been nice."

He rose, somewhat relieved at not having to rent an expensive room. "Let's keep in touch." He certainly wanted to keep picking this woman's brain. The trip wasn't a romantic success, but he no longer wanted to pin his happiness on a woman tied to a child. As he grew older, he realized the stark present never matched the idealized past. But who knew ten years ago the little girl from nowhere had a mind?

As she pulled out onto Highway 2 and headed east, Meagan laughed at her youthful self. Why did she ever think this unsettled middle-aged man was sophisticated much less interesting? He had no direction, no knowledge of how to be a father, much less the willingness to learn. Send Bobby to boarding school? Why would he ever think that she would choose him or any other man over her child? She didn't want Ken Miller to have anything to do with Bobby, even if a DNA test, which she had no doubt Ken would resist, said that Ken was Bobby's father. She shuddered at the thought. Good old Rob had now moved to the third worst father in America.

She glanced at the sky now showing signs of humidity streaming from the south. She knew it would snow and she still had no idea what to do about Bobby's paternity. Her choices had narrowed to keeping the status quo and hoping for the best, or telling the MacLeod's the truth. Neither seemed desirable.

The thought of being Mrs. Leino or Mrs. Miller also made her realize she really didn't want to marry anyone. Having grown up with her father and Don as examples, she loved her independence and her freedom to concentrate solely on Bobby. No, she didn't want to marry. She glanced again at the sky. At least one more blizzard before spring.

CHAPTER 7

Meagan knew something was wrong the minute she heard Jennie's voice on the telephone. Her sister's tone was brittle, her words held together by sobs. "Pop is gone. They found him in a snow bank this morning. He must have gotten confused and got out of his car…"

Meagan knew better. She knew what she had always known, that one day her father would just end his humiliation. She dressed and hurried to her mother's house where everyone cried and pretended the past had never happened. Meagan wanted to start planning but her mother insisted they wait for Don to arrive from Houston.

Waiting for Don was excruciating, giving Meagan time to reflect on her relationship with her father. He was like two people. Her earliest memories were of sitting on his lap while he laughed and told her stories. She also remembered being terrified at his screaming, especially before she realized the spells were sporadic and alcohol-related. On the other hand, she was the fair-haired child; the youngest, the cutest, and most spoiled, making her wonder if the others had resented her. Now that she thought about it, her father's ire was never directed at her. Instead he targeted his wife and son while the three girls hid.

Even as a child, Don fought back while their mother simply cried and begged for mercy. As Don grew, their father should have seen the inevitable as the hostility between father and son became increasingly brutal. She wondered why no one in the tiny hamlet had intervened when Don went to school with the obvious signs of child abuse. She wondered if the neighbors noticed the changes when her father learned to fear Don.

She loved and hated her father in equal measure. If Don had never existed or never challenged their father, she would have lived in a chaotic world forever shifting between parental love and paternal terror. Once Don finally won their increasingly brutal battles, she watched her brother treat their father with such contempt the man shriveled and died inside. Except for his paycheck, he became a nonentity, the invisible member of the family. She would never doubt her father had purposely walked into that snow drift rather than walk back into a house where everyone pretended he simply did not exist.

They buried him on a day when cold Lake winds swirled snow around them before piling it into drifts. The priest from the

Catholic Church, where they almost never attended, was kind enough not only to say a funeral Mass but also give a generic sermon praising the deceased for his faith to his family, friends, and God. The Mass ended with Don going to the pulpit. Meagan inwardly groaned at what he might or might not say.

Don's theme was how he learned self-discipline and responsibility from his father. Since everyone in the church knew his father was a part-time drunk, Meagan thought, they must know Don is speaking in the negative. What did Don learn? He learned that family is everything. Sure, Meagan thought, family is everything as long as everyone does what elder brother says. And, you could throw in a good word about how Pop never abandoned us, even after you threatened him. Then Don started the mantra that would come after every point, "but you know how my father was." Sure, Meagan thought. Trash the man by reminding everyone he was a drunk who beat his wife and son until you got old enough to beat him.

Don learned the importance of protecting the women in the family. Spare us, Meagan thought, waiting for the inevitable "but you know how my father was." To his credit, Don did say his father always worked hard and brought his pay home to their mother. Meagan wondered how many people knew her father would feel Don's fists if he didn't. Don learned the heavy weight of responsibility from his father. Meagan wanted to puke. By the end of the eulogy, everyone who knew the family must have known that Don wasn't praising his father but himself. Meagan thought Don was a complete asshole.

The physical burial would have to wait until the ground was warm enough to dig a grave. So instead of going to the cemetery everyone went directly to the luncheon in the church basement. Gary Guthrie extended his hand. "You can tell your rich friend he can come back. Since his lawyer got Paulette off with time served and probation, her relatives aren't looking for him anymore." Then she watched Gary and Don walk to an empty corner for a quiet conversation. She wondered.

Niles Leino didn't extend his hand. "My brother Todd said to tell you how sorry he is. He couldn't come. He's in the middle of a divorce."

"Tell Todd I said thank you and that I'm sorry to hear about the divorce."

Finally they went to their mother's house, where Don directed his mother on finances and how she was going to live. Jennie and Carol seemed exhausted. Meagan collected Bobby and was about to leave. "I want to talk to you," Don commanded.

"Not now. Tomorrow. Come out in the morning after Bobby goes to school."

♦♦♦

Don was earlier than Meagan expected. He was heading back to Houston, so she figured he'd stop by before going to the airport to get a flight to Chicago. She expected the usual pitch about life under Don's protection in Houston. Maybe she should consider it. Bobby two prospective fathers certainly weren't to her liking and would make a mess of Bobby. She didn't quite understand Rob's continuing closeness with Bobby but she was thankful for his support of the boy. She hoped Don would be brief because after listening to his eulogy yesterday, she had nothing nice to say to him.

Don took off his coat. A bad sign. He asked for coffee. Another bad sign. They sat at the dining room table. "I have a job for you," he began. "Since you didn't finish college, it is low level but there is room for advancement. I'll pay Bobby's tuition and help you until you can get on your feet financially. I told Human Resources you need a month. I know that takes Bobby out of school but HR said we couldn't wait any longer."

"Just like that. How about asking me if I want to move to Houston, if I want to take your charity."

"Don't give me a hard time," his voice rose. "I don't have much time. We've been having this argument since that poor boy was born. I'm tired of it and this is what you are going to do. You've had no problem taking MacLeod's charity. At least I'm family. Mom says your boy talks more and more like he's a MacLeod, that he has people who care about him on that side of his family."

"Is that what is bothering you, Don? That Bobby might grow up thinking well of someone other than almighty Uncle Don?

Don't you think anyone else is capable of doing anything good for him?"

"The boy needs an example of a man, not some weak-ass drunk who beats up on women. Yes, I do object to him thinking he's a real MacLeod because he's a Flannigan and that's what he should be. You keep forgetting he was born on the wrong side of the blanket. That drunk will never really accept him."

"You don't really know Rob any more than you know me." Pent up anger surged into her brain. "You're an arrogant, self-righteous man. Worse than that you're a phony. I know all about you and Gary Guthrie and your little schemes" she lied. "Pauline Pacquette told me all about you."

Meagan had no idea what her brother had to do with Gary Guthrie but Don looked shocked. He stood up. "Pauline is a lying whore and so are you. Don't you think I knew what was going on between you and MacLeod all of these years? Do you think anyone thought you were living virtuously in this house with him? I tried to warn you, tried to tell you, but you're no better than a whore."

She was standing too. "You never knew anything. Nothing at all. I wasn't having sex with Rob MacLeod all those summers or when he was just here. If I was, he wouldn't have been running off to Marquette to see your friend Paulette all of the time. You don't know anything and you never did. I've been having sex with Todd Leino on a regular basis since I was fifteen years old. And I still am. Every time he comes home we spend a day or two rolling around in some motel or in his little trailer out on Fisher's Point. He has it hidden so you can't even see it from the driveway. I keep a toothbrush and a robe out there."

Don looked shocked. "What do you know about Paulette? And Todd Leino? Do you expect me to believe that?"

"Yes, Todd Leino. Remember how he became a savant with a basketball. Well, he is a savant when it comes to sex. Believe me, he taught me enough to keep any man here if I wanted to. You know how long his fingers are? Well, you should see the size of his dick."

Don reached across the table and slapped the side of her face with such force that she fell sideways, hitting her head on a chair as she crumpled. When the blur cleared, she saw the horrified look on her brother's face and went in for the kill. "You're just like him, aren't you? You're just like Pop. Do you beat your wife and slap your daughters too? I could never understand why you hated him so much and now I know. You realized you are just like him and have been trying to escape that fact your whole life. You're a self-righteous prick who probably can't face yourself in the mirror without seeing him. And you didn't have to trash him in that so-called eulogy you gave yesterday."

"I'm not like him. What else could I have done?"

"Shown him a little compassion, left him a little respect in his own house. You could have tried to help him with his problems, treated him like a fellow human being. And you want to be a role model for my son? You're the last thing I'd ever want him to be. Now get out of here before I call the Sheriff and charge you with assault."

"You go to hell, Meagan. As far as I'm concerned, you and your little bastard aren't part of my family anymore."

He reached for his coat. "Who wants to be part of your family? Mom and Jennie cower at the sight of you and Carol ran away as soon as she could. You have never been a big brother," she yelled as he headed for the door. "You were always nothing more than a big bully. You not only ruined Pop's life but all of ours."

The door slammed and then she heard his car race down the driveway. Well, she certainly wouldn't be moving to Houston.

Meagan sat propped against the chair where she had fallen. It was true. Part of her goal in life had always been escaping Don. Being the only one in the family who talked back to him increased Don's need to control her. She knew the only way back into Don's good graces would be to utterly submit to his decisions. She didn't do that at fifteen or sixteen, and she wasn't going to do it now.

She stood and looked into a mirror on her way to the kitchen. Her face was bruised on one side and scratched on the other side. She could always say she had fallen, that no one had been in the house with her. She drank a glass of water and reached for her cell phone on the counter. He didn't answer, so she sat down wondering what to do next.

Rob called back within minutes. "Is Bobby all right?"

"Yes, he's fine. Why do you think something is wrong with Bobby?"

"Because once I realized this was your number, I couldn't think of another reason why you would call me."

"Why do you think I wouldn't call you?"

"As I recall, you hate me."

"Oh that."

"Don't you hate me?"

"Well, maybe, sort of, but that doesn't change the fact that you've always been my best friend, the first person I think of calling when I'm in trouble."

"Why are you in trouble?"

"I just had a fight with Don. He hit me. Knocked me down. My face is cut and bruised."

"Do you want me to get on a plane and defend your honor? You have to remember your brother is a lot bigger and I'm a coward."

"No. I don't want you to fight with Don."

"Maybe I could hire some thugs to work him over."

"Stop that. You just made me smile and it hurts."

"How badly are you hurt?"

"It's all superficial."

"Why did he hit you?"

"He said things I didn't like and I talked back to him. I told him things I probably shouldn't have."

"About me? About us?"

"No. He thinks worse things about us than I could ever tell him. It was about someone else and the way he trashed our father at the funeral. Rob, what am I going to do about Bobby? I've been paralyzed by fear and uncertainty but now I really have to make a decision."

"What do you want to do? Did you find the other fathers? Did you tell them?"

"I found them but I didn't tell them anything. You were right. Neither one of them is good enough to be Bobby's father. I'm sorry I ever told you that you were the shittiest father in the world because you're at least number three from the bottom. Either one of them would be a disaster. I don't want either of them around Bobby."

"And what about me?"

"I'm scared to death you'll get angry at your father and tell him. Worse yet you might tell Bobby."

"I told you I won't. My ultimate revenge against the Old Man is giving another gene pool the MacLeod name and money. He's so fucking proud of being a MacLeod that I can't wait to meet him in hell. That's when I'm going to tell him. I wouldn't tell him when he could still change his will or anything."

"Do you really mean that, Rob? I mean taking on someone else's child is a big thing."

"Meagan, you're such a kind and loving mother that a shitty father like me can only do so much harm. Yes, I'd like to leave someone on this planet who thinks well of me, someone who will be sad when I'm gone. It's not like I'm going to move to the U.P. and take him to baseball practice."

"Bobby and I have to leave here soon. I really want to leave but I don't want to go to Florida with your parents. And I don't know what you are doing in Belize, but I'm pretty sure it would be a bad example for an impressionable boy."

"You're right. I like it here but I sure as shit don't want Bobby seeing me at my worst. I have a small house on the beach, and congenial friends…maybe more like acquaintances. I wouldn't let you come here if you wanted to. It would be the end of our friendship. I have an idea. How about Detroit? Call the Old Man. Play up how you want Bobby to know his Detroit roots and the MacLeod traditions. The Old Man will like that. Tell him you want Bobby to go to a good school like Detroit Country Day or Cranbrook. He has a list. I got kicked out of most of them."

"If he pays Bobby's tuition, I can rent a small apartment and get a job."

"The mother of Bobby MacLeod does not live in just any part of town or take any job. The Old Man is all about appearances. They barely use their perfectly good condo on Lake St. Claire. You can live there. And he'll have to buy you the right car and the right clothes so you can go to the Country Club."

"I don't think I'd fit in with those people at the Country Club."

"What are you talking about? Who do you think were at all those parties during our teenage years? You'll be surprised at how many you already know. Whether you realized it or not, you were in teenage training for the Country Club."

"I'm afraid. Rob, you're really are fond of Bobby, aren't you?"

"I look forward to talking to him because he seems to be the only person around who really likes me. Yes, I'm fond of him. I think I love the kid. I'll be happy to keep being his father."

The sound startled her. "What was that?"

"What?"

"It sounded like an explosion."

"Where? Close to you?"

"Not too close but really loud." She walked into the great room and looked out of the window. "There's smoke, there was an explosion."

"Where?"

"Out on Fisher's Point."

"There's nothing out there, is there?"

"Just an old trailer. Oh shit! Don blew up the trailer."

"Why would Don blow up a trailer? Has he become unhinged?"

"Don isn't the only one who is going to be unhinged by this."

"Meagan, what are you talking about?"

"It's complicated. I'll explain it to you someday."

"Are you in danger? Should you get Bobby and just drive south? I can send you some money."

"No, I don't think I'm in danger. Don should be on his way to the airport. Gives him a great alibi. No one will ever suspect him."

"Call the Old Man. You can handle him. I've seen you do it. Tell him what you want but make him think it is his idea. Call him and then call me back so I can reinforce whatever you said"

"Thanks, Rob. Give me time to collect my thoughts. I will. I always feel better after talking to you."

"Same here, Meagan. Sometimes I think you're as fucked up as I am. But you just have it more together."

She listened to emergency vehicles pass the driveway on their way to Fisher's Point. Maybe Don was crazier than she thought.

♦♦♦

Meagan told Bobby she had tripped in the dining room and hit her face on two chairs. Bobby believed her but the Sheriff wasn't so sure. "Looks like a bruise on one side of your face and a scrape on the other side. Sure someone didn't hit you?"

"No, I was alone. I slipped over there, in the dining room, on the edge of the rug and fell funny. Hit one side on the corner of the chair and then slide down, scraping the other side of my face on the chair next to it."

"Uh, sure." The Sheriff clearly knew the results of a blow when he saw one.

"You know about the explosion yesterday?"

"Yes. I heard it. I saw the smoke out on Fisher's Point."

"Did you know Todd Leino had an old trailer out there?"

"Yes. I did. He mentioned it to me when he told me about buying some property for his retirement. Thought he is a little young to think about retiring."

"Would you say that you and Todd Leino are good friends or anything?"

"Everyone knows we went steady in high school, for three years to be exact. Then we went off to separate colleges where he met his wife."

"Did you know he is getting a divorce?"

"I think I heard something about that at my father's wake. I don't think Todd was there."

"I had a long telephone conversation with Todd this morning. He thinks you blew up his trailer."

"He thinks what?" Meagan was truly surprised. "Why would he think something like that? Why would I do something like that?"

"According to Mr. Leino, you and he have been having a long-lasting and continuous affair and often met at the trailer. He says you are the only other person who knew it was there, so either you blew it up or told someone to do it."

The shock on Meagan's face was genuine. She expected Todd to be upset but not to blame her. "I honestly don't know what to say. I really don't. His allegations are really so far beyond belief. You know I've been living here and, as far as I know, he rarely visits his family. Why would he visit me?"

"He says your affair began in high school and never ended, that he bought the secret trailer so you could be together."

"I'm truly flabbergasted. I mean…I don't know what to say. Believe me, I've barely talked to Todd Leino in all of these years. I mean he was always a bit strange, never quite in tune with reality but this….I mean all of the Leinos are a bit strange but this…."

"I know what you mean. But I have to ask you where you were when the trailer blew up."

"I told you I was here. I heard the explosion and saw the smoke from the great room windows. We have a nice view of the bay and Fisher's Point."

"Was anyone with you?"

"No. I was on the telephone. You can check my cell phone."

"And you were talking to?"

"Rob MacLeod. We were talking about my… our son's education. The elder MacLeods want to send Bobby to a private school. We were discussing it. In fact I mentioned the explosion to him. His number is on my phone. Call him if you like."

"I will. Do you, or did you, have a pair of pink bedroom slippers with bunnies on the end?"

"What? Why would you ask that? I don't. I think I had a pair with bunnies when I was in high school but that was a long time ago. Why do you ask?"

"We found such a slipper in the woods near the remains of the trailer."

"And you think it was blown out of the trailer?"

"No. It didn't show signs of being singed or anything. It was old but hadn't been outside for long. It looked more like someone threw it out of the trailer before the explosion."

"And you think it belongs to me? If it did, Todd has had it for a long time, well over a decade." Fuck, she thought. Don recognized her old slippers, threw one outside, and blew up the trailer. Don wanted her and Todd found out and wanted her blamed for the explosion.

"Are you sure that you didn't have a visitor yesterday, late morning or early afternoon."

"No, I didn't see or hear anyone."

"What about your brother?"

"Don? I saw him after the funeral of course but I think he left for Houston yesterday morning."

"He arrived at the airport shortly after the explosion."

"Then why would you suspect him?"

"Don't necessarily. We know somebody was up there. Tire tracks in fresh mud. A person wouldn't have to be there when the explosion happened."

"They wouldn't?"

"Not if someone just turned on the propane and let the trailer fill with gas. A spark from any of the electronic switches, like the heat coming on, could have triggered the explosion."

"Oh, I see."

"Do you live here alone?"

"With my son. Everyone knows that. Everyone knows everything about everybody around here."

"You might want to move in with your mother or sister for a while."

"Why would I want to do that?"

"Because Todd Leino is on his way here and he seemed very angry with you."

"Oh, Todd wouldn't hurt me. I don't think he'd hurt me. How mad was he?"

"He said you don't want to marry him and you blew up the trailer to get even?"

"Even for what? That doesn't even make sense. I can't imagine what he's talking about. The only discussion I ever had with him about marriage was ten years ago when he told me he was going to marry someone else. Is he so nuts that he thinks I'd wait ten years and then blow his place up? That's crazy."

"It might be crazy but he was angry. Said you'd regret it."

"My God, makes you wonder what goes on in his brain."

"Sure does. You know, you are right. The U.P. is a place where everyone knows everyone else's business but where everyone still has deep, dark secrets. Let me know if you remember any of yours."

"I can't believe you think I did something like this."

"I didn't say I believed it. Just telling you what I was told. Take care of those bruises on your face. I'll let you know if anything changes."

Fuck, Meagan thought as the Sheriff got into his car. He knows. Everyone will know. She had to get Bobby out of the U.P. sooner than she thought.

◆◆◆

"Jennie," the phone was shaking in Meagan's hand. "The Sheriff was just here about that explosion yesterday. He was asking questions about Don."

"Don? Why Don? What happened between you and Don yesterday? He was furious after he saw you."

"I know. I have the bruises on my face to prove it."

"Don?"

"He hit me so hard he bruised one side of my face and I cut the other side when I fell."

"Don? I don't believe it. Did you tell the Sheriff that?"

195

"No, I lied to the Sheriff. Told him Don wasn't here yesterday. There were some tire tracks by the Leino place. I saw the Sheriff's deputy taking photos of the tires of my car and also tracks in the driveway. I should have said Don drove me home last night in case they check the rental Don was driving."

"What were you and Don arguing about? He said some nasty things about you to Mom. Said you are an unrepentant whore and he never wants to be in the same room with you again."

"And of course Mom believes him. Shit, I have to get out of here. I have to take Bobby someplace else."

"Meagan, this doesn't make any sense. What does Todd Leino have to do with you and Don?"

"The Sheriff said Todd is accusing me of having a continuing affair with him and blowing up his trailer."

"Nobody even knew about his trailer. Did you?"

"He says that's where we were having this imagined affair. Maybe Don heard the story."

"I don't believe Don would do anything like that."

"You probably don't think Don would hit me either."

"Well…"

Meagan hung up. So much for getting any help from her mother or her sister.

Meagan tried to be cheerful when Bobby came home. She talked about moving to Detroit, perhaps sooner than later. Once Bobby went to bed, she sat in the little room repeatedly telling herself Todd Leino would not hurt her. If the truth came out, it would not only mortify her family but hurt Bobby as well. She thought of calling Rob again but what could he do? She had no alternative but to call Mr. MacLeod in the morning and suggest she and Bobby move to Detroit where Bobby could attend the private school of Mr. MacLeod's choice. Don was right. She'd been hiding long enough. It was time to start a new life with her son.

In the morning she stood in her bathrobe watching Bobby walk toward the end of the driveway. Then she saw his lunch box next to the door. She stepped outside and yelled to him. They met halfway to the road where she watched the school bus depart before turning back to the house. As she did, Todd's truck careened into the driveway.

Her first instinct was to run which she did but the truck cut her off. Todd jumped out. She tried to run around him toward the house but he grabbed her by the throat and pushed her toward the truck. He opened the door and had her half inside, his long fingers tightening their grip. "Todd, stop you're hurting me."

"Why did you do it?"

"I didn't for God's sake, you're strangling me."

"Tell me or I will hurt you."

She raised one knee and caught him in the groin, hitting him just hard enough to make him step back. "Todd, why would I blow up that trailer? I liked it there. We had good times there. I swear I wouldn't do that."

"Then who did you tell? Who did it?"

"Who did I tell? Who did you tell? You told the Sheriff we've been having an affair! Did you tell him about that motel in Ishpeming too? Fuck, Todd, everyone will know. Your family will know. Your wife will know. Why did you do that? We can't do this anymore. We can never do it again."

He reached for her throat again. "Who did you tell? If you didn't do it, you told somebody about the trailer."

"I told Don. I had a fight with Don and told him. I think he did it."

"You shouldn't have told him. Don is not a nice person."

"I know. Look at my face. This is what he did when I told him. We had an argument about how I live my life and I got angry and told him. You got angry about the trailer and you told the Sheriff, so now everyone in the Sheriff's office knows. The Sheriff asked if you'd been here. He thought you did this to me."

"What did you tell the Sheriff?"

"That I hadn't seen you. I told him I fell rather than telling him it was Don. Why did you say that Don is not a nice person? What do you know about Don?"

"He used to take things to Marquette and Ann Arbor to sell."

"Like what?"

"Gary Guthrie and some of his friends used to grow pot in old cabins. Then they used to steal things from summer homes, break in and steal things. Don took the stuff to Marquette and then to Ann Arbor where he sold it to other students because nobody suspected Don. Sometimes he took girls to Ann Arbor so they could make money too."

"Did he take Paulette Pacquette?"

"I don't know. Probably."

"Why didn't you ever tell me that?"

"You never asked."

He pushed her further into the front seat of the truck. "What are you doing?"

"I want to have sex with you now."

"We can't do that anymore. Everyone will be watching."

"Just one more time. The last time."

"We've said that before."

"No, this is different."

"At least let's go into the house."

"No here in the truck like when we were in high school." He was opening the robe and pushing up her nightgown. "Just one more time."

For once Meagan didn't enjoy the act. All she could think of was of the humiliation if someone came down the driveway, particularly in an age where everyone has a camera on their cell phones. There would be photos of her sprawled out on the front seat of an old truck, one leg on the steering wheel and the other on the back of the seat with Todd banging away, swaying the whole truck to his frantic rhythm. When it was over, she pulled herself up. "Todd, put your arms around me."

"Why? We are finished now."

"Just do it, Todd." He complied. "Todd, I'm going to tell you what you have to do. You have to find another wife. A Yooper. A Finnish girl from a farm. Someone who understands you and your family. You are an important man with a good job. You can give a woman a lot."

"My family says I can't marry you because you have that child."

"Your family is right. I'm not talking about me. Find someone else. Think. Who among the farm folk do you think is attractive? What girl would you like to have sex with?"

"Anna Lalich. She's a little young but she's pretty and has big tits like you. My wife had small ones."

"She's perfect. Send her some flowers with an invitation to dinner. Take her somewhere really nice in Marquette. Take her out every night while you are here. But don't attack her and don't try to have sex with her."

"Why not? That's what I want."

"Because you'll scare her. Invite her to visit St. Louis. Get her a very nice hotel room. Ask her to marry you and then have sex with her. And here is the really important part. Hold her for awhile after you have sex, like you are holding me now."

"Why?"

"Because women like that and then she won't divorce you."

"Did you want that?"

"No, but we're not talking about me. We're talking about some nice girl. Not only hold her after sex but tell her you love her every time you have sex."

"What if I don't that day?"

"Then lie. It's important Todd. Hold her and tell her you love her. And talk to her every day when you get home from work. Tell her at least one little thing about your work."

"Why would she care about my work?"

"Because she'll care about you. Physically, you are the best lover I've ever had. You were probably the best lover your ex-wife will ever have. But you have to do more. You have to tell her that you love her and talk to her. I want you to remember that because I'm going away and won't be here anymore. You are my old life, just like I'm your old life. We can't live in the past any longer. We have to find new lives because our old lives are over. Promise me, Todd. Do what I just told you and you'll be happy, I promise."

"How will you be happy?"

"I don't know the answer to that. I wish I did."

She watched Todd's truck turn out of the driveway and went back into the house. She didn't realize how cold she was until she reached for some coffee. She went into the great room, kicked off her wet slippers, pulled a blanket around her shoulders, and poured some Scotch. She glanced out of the window where the drifts were melting into a patchwork of shiny snow, watery pools and wet mud. That sailboat from last fall was out there again, gliding westward amid the ice flows. Who is that crazy sailor, she wondered, and where did he spend the winter? For a moment she envisioned the boat frozen in a sheet of lake ice, unable to move until the first wisp of spring finally set it free. Hope poured through her veins, a realization spring was also setting her free. Like the sailboat, she had to flee.

She raised the glass while still watching the sailboat float through sun speckled waters and bobbing icebergs, "Rob, I hope this works because I don't know what else to do. I wish you were here." She smiled. "Maybe not. You'd be laughing your head off at that little scene with poor Todd."

She downed the Scotch and reached for her phone. "Good morning, Mr. MacLeod. This is Meagan."

"Hello, Meagan. I've been hoping to hear from you."

"I hope I'm not bothering you. I really appreciate your offer to send Bobby to school in Florida but that is so far away from everything he's used to. I'd like to ask your opinion about something you might think is silly. Would you consider sending Bobby to school in Detroit? That is where the MacLeods have their roots and where the MacLeod name really means something."

"That is a nice idea. Been thinking about that myself."

"I could get a small apartment and…."

"No, no, dear. Your son is a MacLeod. He and his mother can't just live anywhere, especially in Detroit where we are well known. Let me see what I can work out. Glad you've finally come to your senses."

Meagan smiled. Rob sure knew the Old Man. She couldn't wait to call him. Maybe it was just the sunshine or maybe it was Rob's promises, but she suddenly felt safe again, like that boat sailing into sweet waters.

EPILOGUE

The funeral director touched Meagan's black clad arm. "This way, Mrs. MacLeod. You follow the casket along with your son and Mr. MacLeod. Is it all right if your son pushes the wheelchair?"

"Yes. That would be a nice touch."

They lined up in the vestibule waiting for the casket to arrive. A cold spring wind blew across the street from Lake St. Claire. Bobby reached down for her hand. "Are you all right, Mom?"

"I'll get by. What about you?"

She looked up at the tears forming in her son's eyes. "I'm going to miss him terribly. I think even Grandpa will."

"I think Grandpa will be surprised how much he will miss your father."

"I don't know how Grandpa would get along without you, especially since his last stroke."

The procession formed and walked down the long aisle of the neo-Gothic limestone Church long attended by the MacLeod Family. The church was crowded, a tribute to the Old Man and perhaps to Meagan. A lot of Bobby's school mates were there, some even traveled from their respective universities to attend. As they slid into the first pew, Meagan's mind slipped away.

It had gone exactly as Rob had predicted. The Old Man became increasingly enthusiastic about a MacLeod presence in Detroit. A series of phone calls ensued. The elder MacLeod immediately began setting up school interviews at the end of May. He suggested Meagan and Bobby come to Detroit early to prepare.

Rob was leery. "I don't want you alone in that condo with The Old Goat. I don't trust him."

"Really Rob. I hardly think....."

"He's an old lecher. One of the reasons my mother drinks. I notice she won't be there."

"He says she's sick."

"She's in rehab. She's been in rehab more than I have, but give me her years. No, I think I'll fly to Detroit for Bobby's interviews at the end of May. Gives me time to sober up. You do know they expect the parents to be there too."

"I know. Hope I'm not a problem."

"Shit, how can it be you? Nobody knows you. They know me."

"Oh Rob, I hope this doesn't turn out to be a mistake. I still have nightmares of people finding out."

"Are you going to tell them?"

"No."

"That leaves me and I'm not going to tell. I'll see you in Detroit. It will be great to see Bobby again."

"What about me?"

"You're all right but Bobby is terrific."

A week later, Rob called again. "Hey Meagan. There is a complication."

"I knew it."

"We have to get married."

"What?"

"The Old Fart says we have to get married. He's had three calls from old friends saying that Bobby's lack of married parents is the only obstacle to his getting into any school we want. And something about the Country Club not allowing you membership because you are not legally a MacLeod."

"That's crazy. I don't have to go to any Country Club and Bobby just needs one broad-minded school. What's wrong with a public school?"

"Perish the thought! A MacLeod at a public school! The Old Man won't approve anything unless we keep up appearances. It's all about Bobby, you know."

"What kind of marriage are we talking about?"

"Just like always. I'll do what I want and you can do what you want. I'm not the kind who ever comes home for dinner, so you don't have to go through the pretense of making any."

"Bobby and I will live in Detroit; but where will you live?"

"In Belize. Thought it might be nice if we gathered in Florida at Christmas. Kind of an old family tradition. Marriage will strengthen Bobby's claim to MacLeodhood if anything ever happens. It would pretty much guarantee his future."

"If you mean a marriage where we don't necessarily act like a married couple, maybe. I don't want you suddenly telling me what to do."

"And I don't want to ever hear you nag me either."

"When and where is this theoretical union supposed to take place?"

"The Old Man wants it soon and in Florida where the Detroit media won't pick up the suddenness of our union."

"We won't be going on a honeymoon and all that, will we?"

"I love your enthusiasm but we are. I already promised Bobby we'd take him to Disney World. It's going to be a family honeymoon. Do you think you can pull Bobby out of school for a week?"

"You promised Bobby a honeymoon? Not putting too much pressure on me."

"Look at it this way, Meagan. It gets you a claim to the family trust and the next time some bimbo demands marriage, I can say, 'sorry, but 1 already have a wife and can't divorce her.' You could be saving me a lot of grief."

"You sound enthused about this."

"That's because you are the only woman in the world who knows better than to ever try to change me. And I'm the only man in the world who'll think it's funny if you're sleeping around."

"I wouldn't do that to Bobby. I'd be very quiet about it."

"That's good. I don't want you embarrassing my son. That will be my job. So what's your answer?"

"Of course I'll marry you if it assures Bobby's future. Everyone in Thunder Bay, my family included, will say I always was a gold digger. They'll feel sorry for you for being taken in by little old Meagan Flannigan. Proof the summer people aren't so smart after all."

◆◆◆

The minister began the funeral service. Poor Rob. Tears flooded her face as she clutched Bobby's hand. If only she had been there. If only she had known sooner. If only she had asked more questions. If only he had confided in her.

They were married in the living room of the MacLeod house in Palm Beach. Like all things MacLeod, the house bespoke a faded glory. It was a large, pink, Ocean Avenue, Spanish style mansion with elaborate Moorish tiles and trimming. The lot was unusually spacious with a well-landscaped yard and pool. But the inside was dated, even verging on shabby. Meagan wondered whether it was from lack of money or lack of interest. One of the Old Man's friends, who was also a judge, officiated while a dozen other Florida friends attended. Meagan didn't tell her family where or why she was going much less invite them to the wedding. Mr. MacLeod was euphoric but his wife was despondent.

Bobby was thrilled. In twenty-four hours he'd missed school, been on his first airplane, seen his first ocean, and watched his parents get married. After a small luncheon, they drove to Disney World in time to see a bit of the park before going to their two-bedroom suite. Both parents kissed Bobby on the forehead and tucked him into bed.

They walked out into the suite's parlor. "Since it's my wedding day, I think I need a little Scotch."

"Why? It's your fourth wedding. It's my first. I'm the one who needs the drink." He poured two.

"Let's go out on the balcony."

They settled on a large lounge chair and sipped the Scotch. She leaned her head against his shoulder. "Are you sorry you married me yet?"

"Shit, no. The Old Man has disinherited me. That means you and Bobby get everything."

"You can stop that by telling your father the truth about Bobby."

"And let him leave everything to some Scottish charity? I have a better plan. You get control of his estate and I blackmail you into giving me whatever I want."

"You bastard. You married me for my money....or I should say your money. Is that all you want from me? No sweeping me off my feet? No night of grand passion?"

"Is that what you want after all these years? Passion?"

"I could use a little passion in my life and we are married. Let me guess, you plan to go down to the bar and pick up Cinderella after we finish our drink."

"Cinderella isn't my type. The wicked stepmother is more my type. Or maybe a witch. Better yet, a pair of witches."

"Are you planning on bringing this harem of evil up here?"

"Wouldn't want Bobby to find them in the morning?"

"I think Bobby would be traumatized for life if he found you in bed with Cinderella to say nothing of a witch or two?"

"Do you want to consummate the marriage?"

"You are an attractive man and I do have certain needs."

He didn't answer for a while. "I just realized something. I don't have sex with women I like. Only women I don't like. The more I dislike them...."

"Like Paulette? I never had the impression you liked Paulette."

"No, by the end I really didn't. She got high instead of taking her sick child to a clinic. The little girl died. But even after I found out....I just kept banging her while she sometimes literally spit in my face until I'd slug her. I seemed to have known a lot of women like Paulette." He laughed softly. "I don't know if I can perform with a woman I respect."

"Then we'll have our second little secret. Send a strapping workman up here when you go downstairs to find that pair of really wicked witches."

"My son's mother shouldn't do things like that."

"Don't get sanctimonious on me, Rob. I've always been very discreet. So discreet no one ever suspected."

"Suspected what? Who was he? Or should I ask who is he? When was the last time you had sex with a man?"

She hesitated. "Well, maybe I shouldn't tell you this on our wedding night but I'm not going to stop being honest just because we have a marriage license." She gave him a brief history of her relationship with Todd, explained her argument with Don, and described their last encounter with Todd in the front seat of his truck in the most comedic manner she could muster.

"To top it off," she concluded, "he's a brilliant scientist but he's somewhere on the autism spectrum. We barely talked much less ever had a meaningful conversation, unless you count me telling him what to do."

"If you're trying to convince me you have a slutty side, you're doing a good job. Was this guy good in bed?"

"Very good. He was some kind of a genius at a couple of things. Sex was one of them."

"After telling me this, you want me to get into bed with you?"

"You did in Marquette."

"I never quite understood what happened there."

"As I recall, Todd told me he was getting married so I returned to Marquette early and found my Marquette boyfriend in bed with my roommate. The next day I was sitting in my sweats, feeling totally rejected when you showed up. I was crying on your shoulder and you ran your hand up my back, beneath the sweatshirt. You asked where my bra was and I said in the bedroom, that we could get it in the bedroom."

"Yes, it's coming back to me now. We went in the bedroom and you took off your sweatshirt and handed me your bra and asked if I wanted to put it on you. The next thing I knew we were all over the bed. I didn't leave for a week. Maybe you are more than a little slutty."

"What kind of slutty woman do you have in Belize?"

"Why do you think there is a woman in Belize?"

"Because I know you. Come on, I leveled with you."

"I have a live-in housekeeper. She's adequate. She does what I tell her to do. If I told her to have sex with a monkey she'd look at me and say, 'how much more will you pay me to do that?' She keeps pestering me to marry her. She's going to shit when I put our wedding picture in the bedroom."

"If I were you, I wouldn't do that. She may murder you."

"She'd be more likely to murder me if I married her. She'd be my heir, or so she thinks."

"I presume you don't like her much either."

"She's all right. You may be the only woman I've consistently liked. I don't know if I can vouch for that if you keep telling me Todd stories. Did you like him?"

"I've never had sex with anyone I didn't like. I liked him but liked the sex more. I never thought I was in love with him. In fact, he asked me to marry him at one point and I refused. Living with Todd would be a lot lonelier than living alone."

"But what about all that great sex?"

"That probably would have gotten boring with time and respectability. It's been a long day and I'm tired. Maybe you don't find me desirable, but come to bed anyway. You can spend one sexless night. It would be better if Bobby finds us together in the morning."

While he was in the bathroom, she changed into a sheer black nightgown. He stared at her. "What the shit is that?"

"Just a nightgown."

"It's a nightgown like that sweatshirt with two big braless boobs hiding under it. Only that doesn't hide anything. I can see everything."

"There's nothing you didn't see in Marquette. Maybe a little more of it. I'll put on wooly pajamas if you like."

He pulled back the covers. "You planned this didn't you? You didn't just come up with a nightgown like that."

"I didn't have a plan. Just if this nightgown didn't have any effect on you, I'd give up."

"You win. Just take it off and get into bed. And while we're there, but only while we're there, call me 'honey.' Never call me 'honey' any place other than in bed."

She laughed. "Well, honey, I don't think I'm the only one who is going to win. This honey is going to make you feel like a whole new man."

"Fuck. You're doing a real number on me, and you know it. Just shut up and get on top of me."

"Fuck is what I aim to do, honey."

"Was that all right," he asked

"Of course, it was all right," she answered. "Why would you even ask?"

"The way you talked about that other guy."

"It was better than with Todd because I feel something for you I never felt for him, or anyone else. If you would have gone limp in the middle of it, you'd still be better because I've always had a very strange emotional attachment to you."

"Are you trying to make me feel good?"

She suddenly realized she was back in her teenage job of making Rob feel better about himself. "Since when did I start lying to you? I've just told you the intimate secrets of my secret sex life. Maybe I shouldn't have."

"Did he teach you to tighten those muscles that way?"

"I don't know. I guess so. He got instructions from medical books."

His laughter broke any tensions. "What kind of guy gets sex directions from medical books?"

"I told you he was a little weird."

"As long as you are being so fucking honest, what you expect from this marriage? I hope you're not going to renege on our agreement."

"I don't want a conventional marriage anymore than you do. Even as a little girl I never wanted to get married, to have some man telling me what to do, just like you don't want some woman nagging you. But that doesn't mean I don't have feelings for you."

She hesitated. " I know in five days you're going back to screwing a woman you don't really like, because you like screwing women you don't really like, although you didn't have any trouble screwing me just now. Either I'm an exception or you're lying. I'd like to think I'm the exception, so I will. A lot of people might find our relationship sick, but I like it the way it is. And just because I don't want an ordinary marriage, doesn't mean I don't like to screw a man's brains out every now and then. Either I'm nuts or I love you in some weird way. Probably both."

"So what do I really want in this marriage, besides giving Bobby some respectability?" she continued. "I want the friendship and honesty we've always had but with benefits. I would like you to visit us three or four times a year, maybe for a week at a time, to bond with Bobby and remind me of the sex I'm missing but you're not. In return I'll never show up in Belize, unless there is an emergency. You can do whatever you want in Belize. You can tell me what goes on there or not. I'll never ask. But when you are with Bobby and me, I would like you to act like a husband both at the country club and in the bedroom."

"And what will you do when I'm not around?"

"I'll be alright. After all, I've spent the last decade with just irregular visits from Todd. And if I'm not alright, I know a lot better than to start sleeping around in the MacLeod social circle. Your father's private investigator talked to everyone in Thunder Bay and didn't come up with a hint of Todd. Just be home for Christmas, Easter, and the 4th of July or whenever you want. I'll be looking forward to MacLeod Family holidays in a whole new way."

"Shit, I wasted a lot of good years by not screwing you when we were kids. If I only knew then…."

"Now go to sleep. Bobby will be up early in the morning."

"I knew it. Marriage makes women naturally bossy. You're already getting demanding and putting pressure on me."

She snuggled up against him. "Honey, I want to put all kinds of pressure on you in all kinds of places."

"O.K., Meagan, you can cut the slutty act. You have a deal. I can live with acting like a proper husband for a week every three or four months. But I don't want you embarrassing me or Bobby either."

"I promise."

"How did you manage to get slutty all of a sudden?"

"I try, Rob. I try."

At the airport, Rob shook Bobby's hand but looked at Meagan. "Best honeymoon I've ever been on and I've been on a few." Then he boarded a plane for Belize.

♦♦♦

Bobby gave the eulogy. As she watched her twenty-year-old son walk to the pulpit, Meagan still wondered. He had Rob's name and inheritance. His six feet, two inches of height suggested Todd although Don's height could explain his nephew being taller than his legal father and grandfather. His mind suggested Ken, a good student with the making of a great scholar. He was in his last year at Yale and was going to Oxford on a Fulbright in the fall. But whatever else he was, he was hers. He had her coloring, her features, and her personality and none of the ticks of his potential fathers.

He began. "My father was not a conventional person and we did not have a conventional relationship, at least in terms of him showing up at the dinner table every night. In fact, I barely knew the man during the first years of my life. But once we met, something magical happened; an instant bond that will never die. My mother doesn't know this, but ever since I was nine years old, I called my father every morning to ask him how he was. It was our secret. Sometimes I obviously woke him or he hadn't been asleep. Then I would apologize for bothering him to which he'd say, 'never apologize, son, because I'm lucky someone calls me every morning. I'm happy you care. I don't think anyone else does.' I'd tell him that wasn't true because Mom cared. Often he added 'you are the bright spot in my life.' What little boy or growing man doesn't want to hear that? Then, in the late afternoons or early evenings, we usually had some skype time during which he asked about my day and gave me fatherly advice. One of the funniest incidents in my life was his trying to explain the birds and the bees over the Internet. I learned not to be too inquisitive about his days because I realized he had faults. Slowly, listening to my peers, I began to realize that, although we were only physically together three or four times a year, I had a closer and better relationship with my father than most of those around me. I never, ever doubted that he loved me or had my best interests in his heart."

He continued. "Last night I thought about the advice he repeated over the years. Phrases jumped out like 'study hard because nobody can take knowledge away from you.' Or, 'don't waste your life playing. Find a job or a cause you love and pursue it. That will keep you out of a lot of trouble.' He often told me 'take care of the people who love you because they are the best things you will ever have.' His constant refrain was 'make me proud of you, son, and never follow my example. Be a better man than I am.' In lots of ways, I don't think there could have been a better man than my father. I love him dearly.

Bobby wiped a tear from his cheek. "He talked about my mother too. He always told me 'do whatever your mother tells you because she's the kindest, smartest woman I know and she loves you better than anything.' Sometimes he told me 'some people thought I was crazy marrying a little Yooper girl but she's the best thing that ever happened to the MacLeods. She's shaped us up and given us a little class. Thank God every night she's on your side.' I do, Mom, and I never doubted how much he loved you."

This time Meagan brushed tears aside. "So in conclusion, I'd like to say that I will miss my father every day for the rest of my life. I know. I've heard a lot of stories about his misbehavior around the Country Club, but I saw the better side of him. I saw love, understanding, and compassion. I even saw his self-awareness of his flaws and his desire not to pass them on to me. Even if he didn't come home for dinner every night, I never doubted the strength of our mutual bond. Whatever else Rob MacLeod was, he was a wonderful father."

Meagan couldn't help breaking down in tears and wishing Don was there to hear a son's loving eulogy.

♦♦♦

Meagan greeted people on the steps of the Church. Her life in Detroit had happened so fast that she could barely believe it.

The first year had been miserable as she and Bobby adjusted. She enrolled in some classes and bonded with her sister, Carol, who lived in a middle class suburb. They often sat on the patio outside the MacLeod condo looking out at the marina and rehashing old stories one or the other of them had forgotten. They particularly agreed on Don. Carol gave her a sense of still being part of a family of her own and news of the U.P. For years she rarely talked to Jennie and never to her mother or Don.

During her second year in Detroit, she'd become active in Bobby's school and at the Country Club. Let people call her "the Yooper," she often referred to herself that way. Beat them at their own game, she always thought, and don't care what they think. The same year Rob's mother died after falling down a flight of stairs. The Old Man talked about moving to Detroit but didn't.

Rather quickly the elder MacLeod had a series of strokes leaving him incapacitated. Meagan flew to Florida to take care of him. Much to her dismay, Meagan suddenly had the Old Man's power of attorney and control of the MacLeod Family Trust. She told Rob to come home and handle things. "Didn't I tell you that's why I married you? You are in charge. You're the only person I trust. Except Bobby and he's still too young."

"But it's your money and your father, Rob."

"It's our money and you know the Old Man and I would kill each other. Maybe I'll have to remind you more often we're married. But while we're on the subject, I really would like an allowance from the Trust."

"Just tell me how much."

At Rob's urging, she had taken some finance courses and hired some of her professors to go through and explain the trust and its investments. Following their advice, she sold the house in Palm Beach for just under $50 million, almost doubling her available capital. She bought a $5 million dollar condo on South Ocean overlooking the Atlantic. The Old Man objected until she patiently explained they were only modest millionaires and not billionaires, so could no longer maintain the lifestyle of his youth. She hired health care workers, but brought the Old Man to Detroit for the warmer months so she could personally oversee his care. Once Bobby was at Yale, she spent her winters in Florida with the elder MacLeod.

She formed the Faded Glory Corporation to deal with the money-eating estate in the U.P. She didn't like the name but Rob insisted, muttering about some kind of tribute to his mother. She hired Jim to oversee a renovation of the old mansion into an inn and the party barn into a community center. She leased the woodlands to a logging company but the real money was in the lakeshore and its views. A series of condos sold briskly along with mandatory memberships in the Faded Glory Community Association.

She eventually let Jim hire Jennie, leading to a partial thaw in their sisterly relationship. Meagan glanced at them now, talking to Carol and her husband. She would like to think that they were there because they were her family but she suspected it was because they were her employees.

At first, people in Thunder Bay, where she now spent part of every summer in the family apartment in the Faded Glory Inn, didn't seem to know how to treat her. But as the years went by and she melded into the society of summer people, she became very respectfully Mrs. MacLeod. She reconciled with her mother, but only saw Don at their mother's funeral. They did not speak.

Throughout the years she spoke to Rob with increasing frequency, often daily. She always ran any ideas past him, knowing he would ultimately tell her to do whatever she wanted. After all, he'd say, the MacLeod Family Trust, of which he was now a full member, had doubled its assets and was no longer bleeding money. They both understood such conversations signaled her respect for him and his trust in her. They spent a lot of his annual visits in their bedroom, alternating between long conversations and physical contact. She consciously kept his visits pleasant and peppered with the kind of sex he liked. "Do you know how I'm going to spend my retirement," he asked.

"Retirement from what?"

"Full time partying. Maybe I'll slow down. Maybe I'll move back to the States and spend most of my time on top of you."

"Can't wait."

Carol approached her as she got into the limousine for the trip to the cemetery. "You'll never guess who called yesterday. Don. He wanted to know if I thought he should come."

"Here? To Rob MacLeod's funeral?"

"I told him not unless he was prepared to apologize for hitting you and calling you names. He hung up."

"We both know Don is incapable of ever admitting he's wrong about anything. And I'm never going to apologize to him for anything. Maybe we're too much alike."

"I just heard from Jennie that he lost his job. Maybe he needs money."

"Maybe. If he does, let me know. I can send him something through you on the condition he never knows who it came from. I wouldn't like to see his long-suffering wife and children do without."

"I knew you'd say something like that."

♦♦♦

The trip to the cemetery brought self-recriminations. She should have known. She should have guessed. She should have gone to Belize in spite of what she had promised and what Rob subsequently told her. In retrospect she had known something was wrong but just didn't realize what.

The first hint had come about two years ago. She'd watched him from bed as he turned from opening the draperies blocking the bright Easter sun rising over the Atlantic. "Hey," she teased, "you're getting a little pouch where your flat stomach used to be. And you have the suggestion of breasts. Either you're getting a little tubby or you're pregnant,"

He didn't seem amused. "Very funny, Meagan."

"Oh Rob, it's just middle age. You're over forty years old now."

"I know and it makes me tired. I think I need a Bloody Mary for breakfast."

"Just don't overdo it."

"Are you telling me what to do?"

"Just making a suggestion. Fuck but you're crabby lately."

"I'm just tired. Maybe it is middle age."

When he arrived in Detroit the following 4th of July, she noticed he'd lost a little weight. In the bedroom, his stomach still seemed extended. "Rob, are you feeling well?"

"Just because I couldn't perform…"

"I don't care about that. I care about your health. Maybe you should see a doctor."

"I did. In Belize City."

"And?"

"Belize has a crappy medical system."

"That's not an answer."

"The doctor said I've picked up some kind of tropical virus. It's nothing."

"Maybe you should get a second opinion while you're here."

"Maybe I will. I'm sure it will go away once it runs its course." In retrospect she didn't know if he saw a doctor or not.

At Christmas he did see a doctor in Florida. He seemed exhausted when he returned. "So?"

"He just confirmed the diagnosis."

"A tropical virus?"

He hesitated. "Yes, a tropical disease. Just don't tell Bobby about it."

"Is there some treatment?"

"Some but it's pretty drastic."

"That doesn't sound very good."

"It's fine. It will eventually go away. Don't nag me. Get me a Scotch and let's have a little fun."

At Easter he called at the last minute to say he would not be coming to Florida.

"Why? What is wrong?

"Nothing."

"Oh, you're just tired of Bobby and me." She wondered if he was once again in love with love and wondered if he would tell her about whomever she was.

"Cut the crap Meagan. You sound like every other woman in the world. I don't want to hear it. I'm not in a mood to hear it!"

"Then tell me what is wrong."

"It's this thing. This virus."

"You mean it's not gone?" He never mentioned it in his calls and texts.

"It keeps coming back. I'm in the hospital in Belize City."

"I'll fly down there."

"No you won't. Besides, I'm getting out tomorrow."

"I'll come to your house and take care of you."

"I have a woman to take care of me and she wouldn't like having you around."

Meagan was stunned by the rejection. "I guess that put me in my place." She was sure there was another woman, either a new housekeeper or someone else. Well, she reasoned, knowing Rob it wouldn't last forever.

"Just tell Bobby I have the flu and will see him at Christmas." He hung up.

The limousine pulled past the iron gates and traversed the narrow lanes that led to a large plot with the angel topped granite monument marking the last resting place of the Clan MacLeod. Meagan almost tripped as she started toward the open gravesite covered by a canopy and surrounded by chairs. She looked back to be certain the funeral director was taking Mr. MacLeod's wheelchair out of the car and helping the Old Man get into it. Bobby pushed him behind her.

Meagan had questioned Bobby about his communications with Rob. Apparently for the past year, they'd been communicating by text rather than face to face. Rob had explained that, with his and Bobby's busy schedules, it made more sense. Meagan pushed Rob's health aside. Surely if it was serious he'd tell her.

She wanted Rob to come for Thanksgiving but he said he'd stay longer at Christmas instead. Maybe he'd move back to the States and repeated his earlier comment about retiring. She laughed and told him she'd be holding him to at least two weeks at Christmas.

She didn't recognize the number but knew the international code for Belize. "Is this Mrs. MacLeod? Mrs. Meagan MacLeod?" The voice had a British accent. "My name is Anthony Richards. I'm a friend of Rob's."

"Yes, Mr. Richards." Her heart seemed to stop. "Is anything wrong?"

"Rob doesn't want me to call you but he's in the hospital in Belize City."

"Is it that pesky virus again?"

"Virus? Is that what he told you?"

"What didn't he tell me?"

"He has an advanced cirrhosis of the liver. He's in bad shape and the medical services here are not that good. His friends have been encouraging him to go back to the States for treatment and quit drinking. He'd quit for a day or two but then he'd go back to it. We thought you knew."

She told Bobby she'd pick him up for the trip to Belize City. She called a doctor she knew from the Country Club who said he'd make an immediate appointment for Rob with Detroit's leading specialist. He suggested a medevac flight but Meagan had already chartered a plane. She'd call him after she had a better notion of Rob's condition. The doctor's wife, listening on the extension, said she would call the Senator's wife. Someone from the American Embassy would undoubtedly pick them up at the airport.

Meagan took one look at Rob and knew why he hadn't come home. She also knew she was probably already too late. He was a yellow skeleton except for his swollen abdomen and legs.
As an obviously shocked Bobby reached for Rob's hand, she texted the doctor who said he'd arrange the medical evacuation for the morning.

"Why in the shit didn't you tell me, Rob?" She was at once angry and devastated.

"What good would that have done? I knew I couldn't stop drinking, so figured I'd spare you and Bobby the misery. You shouldn't have brought Bobby. I didn't want him to see me this way."

"I can't do this alone, Rob. And Bobby would have never forgiven me if I hadn't told him."

"Why didn't you tell me?" Bobby struggled with his tears. "I would have come and gotten you. I would have taken you home."

"We are taking you home," Meagan said. "Jake Stollar is arranging a medical evacuation in the morning and the best medical care in Detroit. That's all you need, Rob, is decent medical care."

He closed his eyes and then opened them again. "A new liver is what I really need."

"We'll get you that too."

"There you go Meagan, always trying to save me. You're always so good to me and I always did such shitty things to you."

"No you didn't. You've given me everything. I'm the very respectable Mrs. MacLeod with a very wonderful son."

"You'd have landed on your feet one way or another. You always knew what you were doing. Maybe without me you would have found yourself a decent husband."

"You know me better than that, Rob."

He turned his head toward Bobby, his voice soft. "You are the best thing that ever happened to me. I would have never known unconditional love without you."

"Dad, that's a terrible thing to say in front of Mom."

"She understands, Bobby. Your mother always understood. She took a leap of faith in giving me a child and knows how grateful I am. She saved the MacLeods from themselves. She knows things. She knows secrets that should never see the light of day. And she knows I never want them revealed. I want you always to love me."

"I love you, Dad. You're the best father in the world."

"Then I've broken the MacLeod curse." He turned toward Meagan. "I told you I could do it. I want Bobby to always think I was the best father I could be."

Meagan smiled but Bobby spoke. "Why wouldn't I, Dad?"

"Just the ramblings of an old man. I don't know what I'm saying. I spite of everything, I'm glad you came. And I'm glad your mother came too."

He closed his eyes again. "If you can bribe a nurse, I'd like another pain killer and a few hours of sleep."

Rob died shortly before dawn with Meagan and Bobby by his side.

After the initial shock, the man from the Embassy said he would arrange for the body to be flown to Detroit if Meagan would give him the name of a funeral home. In the meantime, he had secured hotel rooms and advised them to get some rest. Meagan asked if she could visit Rob's house in the afternoon. Bobby wanted to go with her but she convinced him he needed to stay in

Belize City to see to his father's transport. She didn't want her son to come face to face with Rob's other life.

Meagan sat in the relative cool of Rob's house. Someone brought her a drink. She asked to see the housekeeper who, the man from the Embassy said, claimed to be Rob's wife. The woman was probably in her mid twenties, short, dark, and buxom with dark eyes flickering between sadness and fear. "How long were you Rob's mistress?"

"Five years. We were married for the last two."

"You were not married. I've been married to him for ten years. Your marriage was not valid." She didn't argue, so perhaps she knew the truth. "Were you good to him?"

"I tried to be."

"Was he good to you?"

She hesitated. "Not always."

"Did he hit you?"

"Sometimes."

Meagan thought the woman had earned her keep. "Did you steal from him?"

Again she weighed her answer. "He had much. We have little. Sometimes I needed to help feed my family."

Meagan understood the impoverished living among the wealthy; watching a life she could probably never have. "I presume you want money from me." The housekeeper nodded. "Tell me what happened. How long he had been sick?"

"I do not know. He was drinking more and more. Then he seemed tired all of the time. I noticed some bruises didn't seem to heal. He went to a doctor in Belize City. He didn't drink for two days and then he drank for two days and nights without sleeping. He became mean. I could see he was sick but what could I do? He'd go to the hospital and not drink for a few days but then he'd start again. After he hit me a couple of times, I told him I was leaving."

"Is that when he went through a marriage ceremony with you?"

"Yes, he promised I would inherit this house...and some money."

"The house did not belong to him. It belongs to a family trust I control, as does any money outside of this house. I presume you already have any money that was in this house."

"I should have known some rich American woman would come and take everything. I should have known he was lying so I would take care of him."

"You were not my husband's first mistress here." She nodded. "Who was the other woman or women and where are they now?"

"I only know of Esmeralda. He grew angry one day and told her to go away. So she left. She is now married and has two children by her husband. I am her cousin. She sent me to take care of him. We also cleaned his house, washed his clothes, and made his food."

"And you have no children."

"No. I tried but no."

"I hope he never really hurt you."

"No. He screamed more than anything. He slapped me a couple of times but did not really beat me like some men do."

"That's good. What can you tell me about his friends?"

The man from the Embassy intervened. "I can give you a reports on his friends. A varied groups with pretty much the same problems. One of them has been hanging around. I think he'd like to offer his condolences. His name is Anthony Richards. British."

"Yes, he called me. I'll talk to him alone."

Anthony Richards went through the usual sorrowful clichés. "Sit down and have a drink with me. I want to thank you for calling me. He'd have died alone if you hadn't. Tell me about Rob's life here." He looked a bit startled. "You can tell me everything. I knew about his weaknesses and his women. We were friends long before we were married."

"I know. He talked about you. He said he wished he could be the husband you deserved as well as a proper father to his son. He really loved that boy, talked about him all of the time."

"He probably was a better husband than I deserved, and he was certainly the kind of husband I wanted. And he was a good father. Rob always sold himself short. We were very lucky to have him in our lives. Just tell me about what his life was like here."

Anthony Richards, whose crisp tones suggested the British upper class, painted the picture Meagan expected. Rob slept late, spent his afternoons on the beach drinking with a group of expats. By sunset more gathered around a fire on his beach for impromptu dinners and more drinking supplemented with drugs. Rob was the proverbial soft touch who provided food, drinks, and drugs as well as small loans. He loved being around congenial friends. Meagan thought of the beach parties he so loved in their teenage years. Rob was truly Peter Pan who found eternal boyhood in Belize.

"The woman he lived with?"

"She tried to placate him when he was really drunk and took care of him in the end. I think she was here for what she could get. I think she knew he was already married when they went through that ceremony but thought she might inherit something anyway. And I don't think he cared about her as a person. He just wanted to be sure he had a caretaker."

"Thank you for being so truthful. It rings true. I just wish you had called me six months earlier."

"He was so far gone, I'm not sure that would have done any good. We'll all miss him."

"I will too."

Back in the limousine Meagan turned to the man from the Embassy. "I'll need a trustworthy local lawyer before we leave tomorrow. I want to give the house to his housekeeper or whatever she was. Plus $20,000 U.S. money. And find Esmeralda, his former mistress. I want her to have $20,000 too."

The man looked shocked. "Madam, it is hardly necessary and highly unusual."

Meagan was hot, tired, and uncomfortable. She couldn't wait to get to a hotel room where she could crank up the air conditioning, take a long shower, have a late dinner with Bobby, and cry. "It isn't much. Maybe I should do more. My husband was unusual in lots of way but he certainly wasn't cheap. He would have approved. And I wasn't asking your opinion or inquiring about local customs. Excuse me for being so blunt but I've become accustomed to people doing what I tell them when I tell them."

She could see the disapproval in his eyes but she didn't care. "Whatever you say, Mrs. MacLeod. Whatever you say."

♦♦♦

She could barely look at the hole in the ground with the casket perched above it. Tears not only ran down her face but Bobby's and the Old Man's as well. She couldn't help but think of the irony of the situation. Someday soon the MacLeod Trust would belong to little Meagan Flannigan and her bastard son of uncertain paternity. Somewhere, Rob had to be laughing. He'd kept the secret and now only she knew of their terrible conversation.

For years she'd struggled with the questions of when and what to tell Bobby. She understood Rob's deathbed wish that Bobby never know. She agreed. She wouldn't tell him anything. After listening to Bobby's eulogy she realized they were father and son by choice if not by nature. Theirs was the true love story here. Maybe someday Bobby' children or grandchildren would look at their DNA test results and wonder why they didn't have any Scottish ancestry. By that time, it wouldn't make much difference.

She also understood while she and Rob loved each other in a way, living in continual intimacy would have resulted in monumental clashes. Used to having things his own way, Rob would have blown up at any signs of nagging which she would have eventually done because she too wanted things her way. She'd have answered anger with anger, especially when he would have told her what she could and could not do. Bobby would have just been another kid with bitterly divorced parents instead of one with loving parents living in different countries. Living apart was a mutual act of kindness that saved their deep friendship.

She knew people, her family included, would say she had always been after the MacLeod money She didn't think so. She'd never thought about inheriting the MacLeod money. All those years living at the MacLeod summer cottage, she'd only hoped for Bobby's college tuition. She didn't initiate her marriage; that was the Old Man's idea. When she did marry Rob, she'd only presumed the equivalent of her previous salary, a small allowance to take care of her personal needs. What she always wanted was independence and the means to raise her son. Thanks to Rob she now had both in abundance, but she would have achieved a smaller measure by herself. All she'd ever needed was a decent job outside the U.P. paying enough to provide Bobby with shelter and supplement his education. But the world would never believe it.

The minister finished the last prayers. As he turned to leave, Meagan rose abruptly.

"Excuse me," she said. "I hadn't planned to say anything but feel compelled to do so. Bobby was right. He had an unconventional but loving relationship with Rob. And as most of you know, Rob and I had a unconventional marriage but one that suited both of us."

"That was appropriate because I'm not burying a conventional husband. In fact, I rarely thought of Rob as my husband. Our relationship began in the U.P. when I was just fifteen…but lied and said I was sixteen… and he was eighteen. We started talking one afternoon and never stopped. We frequently said to each other, 'I feel so much better after talking to you.' He was my confidant and I was his. We knew each other's secrets but never judged each other. So today I'm not burying my husband. I'm burying someone more important. I'm burying my best friend."

"Of course, after some years our relationship changed and we had a son. Bobby and I didn't see Rob for some time but the minute he reappeared we talked as easily as we ever did. I told him things most wives would never tell their husbands. And I knew the secrets most men hide from their spouses. Ours might have been the most completely honest marriage in the history of the institution. It worked for us, not because we were strange...well, we might have been a little strange...but because we both married our best friend and kept that friendship the focus of our relationship."

"Mutual respect, complete honesty, and real concern held that friendship together. Rob tried to hide it but, beneath everything, he was a good and loving man. Don't think me naïve. I knew his many faults and weaknesses better than most. He knew them too. Unlike most of the men in my life, Rob possessed a high degree of self-awareness that made him understanding and compassionate towards others. If you think past...shall we say his fun-loving ways... he was never mean or stingy. He went out of his way to make other people feel comfortable. He was generous and forgiving because he understood weakness in others, myself included. I was lucky to have him as my best friend."

"I'd like to end by paraphrasing something he once said to me during a rather bad moment in our long relationship. I hope he can hear me. I think I love you, Rob. I always will."

ABOUT THE AUTHOR

M.L. Sullivan has been a college professor, high school teacher, artist, writer, chef, and "CIA agent" stationed in Upper Michigan. In her own mind, she lives with her handsome husband and three precocious children on a luxurious estate at an undisclosed location. She specializes in wry humor and pure fiction.

Made in the USA
Columbia, SC
08 September 2019